SARAH LEE BROWN FLEMING

HOPE'S HIGHWAY

CLOUDS AND SUNSHINE

AFRICAN-AMERICAN WOMEN WRITERS, 1910–1940

HENRY LOUIS GATES, JR. *General Editor*

Jennifer Burton *Associate Editor*

SARAH LEE BROWN FLEMING

HOPE'S HIGHWAY

CLOUDS AND SUNSHINE

Introduction by
JACQUELYN Y. McLENDON

G.K. HALL & CO.
An Imprint of Simon & Schuster Macmillan
New York

Prentice Hall International
London   Mexico City   New Delhi   Singapore   Sydney   Toronto

Introduction copyright © 1995 by Jacquelyn Y. McLendon

G.K. Hall & Co.
An Imprint of Simon & Schuster Macmillan
866 Third Avenue
New York, NY 10022

Library of Congress Catalog Card Number: 94-12993

Printed in the United States of America

Printing Number
1 2 3 4 5 6 7 8 9 10

Library of Congress Cataloging-in-Publication Data

Fleming, Sarah Lee Brown.
Hope's Highway ; and, Clouds and sunshine / Sarah Lee Brown Fleming.
p. cm — (African American women writers, 1910–1940)
Includes bibliographical references (p.).
ISBN 0-8161-1625-3 (alk. paper)
1. Afro-Americans—Literary collections. I. Fleming, Sarah Lee Brown. Clouds and sunshine. 1994. II. Title. III. Title: Clouds and sunshine. IV. Series.
PS3511.L445A6 1994
818'.5209—dc20   94-12993
                                                               CIP

This paper meets the requirements of ANSI/NISO Z39.48-1992 (Permanence of Paper).

CONTENTS

GENERAL EDITORS' PREFACE

The past decade of our literary history might be thought of as the era of African-American women writers. Culminating in the awarding of the Pulitzer Prize to Toni Morrison and Rita Dove and the Nobel Prize for Literature to Toni Morrison in 1993, and characterized by the presence of several writers—Toni Morrison, Alice Walker, Maya Angelou, and the Delany Sisters, among others—on the *New York Times* Best Seller List, the shape of the most recent period in our literary history has been determined in large part by the writings of black women.

This, of course, has not always been the case. African-American women authors have been publishing their thoughts and feelings at least since 1773, when Phillis Wheatley published her book of poems in London, thereby bringing poetry directly to bear upon the philosophical discourse over the African's "place in nature" and his or her place in the great chain of being. The scores of words published by black women in America in the nineteenth century—most of which were published in extremely limited editions and never reprinted—have been republished in new critical editions in the forty-volume *Schomburg Library of Nineteenth-Century Black Women Writers*. The critical response to that series has led to requests from scholars and students alike for a similar series, one geared to the work by black women published between 1910 and the beginning of World War Two.

African-American Women Writers, 1910–1940 is designed to bring back into print many writers who otherwise would be unknown to contemporary readers, and to increase the availability of lesser-known texts by established writers who originally published during this critical period in African-American letters. This series implicitly acts as a chronological sequel to the Schomburg series, which focused on the origins of the black female literary tradition in America.

In less than a decade, the study of African-American women's writings has grown from its promising beginnings into a firmly established field in departments of English, American Studies, and African-American Studies. A comparison of the form and function of the original series and this sequel illustrates this dramatic shift. The *Schomburg Library* was published at the cusp of focused academic investigation into the interplay between race and gender. It covered the extensive period from the publication of Phillis Wheatley's *Poems on Various Subjects, Religious and Moral* in 1773 through the "Black Women's Era" of 1890–1910, and was designed to be an inclusive series of the major early texts by black women writers. The Schomburg Library provided a historical backdrop for black women's writings of the 1970s and 1980s, including the works of writers such as Toni Morrison, Alice Walker, Maya Angelou, and Rita Dove.

African-American Women Writers, 1910–1940 continues our effort to provide a new generation of readers access to texts—historical, sociological, and literary—that have been largely "unread" for most of this century. The series bypasses works that are important both to the period and the tradition, but that are readily available, such as Zora Neale Hurston's *Their Eyes Were Watching God*, Jessie Fauset's *Plum Bun* and *There is Confusion*, and Nella Larsen's *Quicksand* and *Passing*. Our goal is to provide access to a wide variety of rare texts. The series includes Fauset's two other novels, *The Chinaberry Tree: A Novel of American Life* and *Comedy: American Style*, and Hurston's short play, *Color Struck*, since these are not yet widely available. It also features works by virtually unknown writers, such as *A Tiny Spark*, Christina Moody's slim volume of poetry self-published in 1910, and *Reminiscences of School Life, and Hints on Teaching*, written by Fanny Jackson Coppin in the last year of her life (1913), a multi-genre work combining an autobiographical sketch and reflections on trips to England and South Africa, complete with pedagogical advice.

Cultural studies' investment in diverse resources allows the historic scope of the *African-American Women Writers* series to be more focused than the *Schomburg Library* series, which covered works written over a 137-year period. With few exceptions, the authors included in the *African-American Women Writers* series wrote their major works between 1910 and 1940. The texts reprinted include all of the works by each particular author that are not otherwise readily obtainable. As a result, two volumes contain works originally published after 1940. The Charlotte Hawkins Brown volume includes her book of etiquette published in 1941, *The Correct Thing To Do—To Say—To Wear*. One of the poetry volumes contains Maggie Pogue Johnson's *Fallen Blossoms*, published in 1951, a compilation of all her previously published and unpublished poems.

Excavational work by scholars during the past decade has been crucial to the development of *African-American Women Writers, 1910–1940*. Germinal bibliographic sources such as Anne Allen Shockley's *Afro-American Women Writers 1746–1933* and Maryemma Graham's *Database of African-American Women Writers* made the initial identification of texts possible. Other works were brought to our attention by scholars who wrote letters sharing their research. Additional texts by selected authors were then added, so that many volumes contain the complete oeuvres of particular writers. Pieces by authors without enough published work to fill an entire volume were grouped with other pieces by genre.

The two types of collections, those organized by author and those organized by genre, bring out different characteristics of black women's writings of the period. The collected works of the literary writers illustrate that many of them were experimenting with a variety of forms. Mercedes Gilbert's volume, for example, contains her 1931 collection, *Selected Gems of Poetry, Comedy, and Drama, Etc.*, as well as her 1938 novel, *Aunt Sara's Wooden God*. Georgia Douglas Johnson's volume contains her plays and short stories in addition to her poetry. Sarah Lee Brown Fleming's volume combines her 1918 novel *Hope's Highway* with her 1920 collection of poetry, *Clouds and Sunshine*.

The generic volumes both bring out the formal and thematic similarities among many of the writings and highlight the striking individuality of particular writers. Most of the plays in the volume of one-acts are social dramas whose tragic endings can be clearly attributed to miscegenation and racism. Within the context of these other plays, Marita Bonner's surrealistic theatrical vision becomes all the more striking.

The volumes of *African-American Women Writers, 1910–1940* contain reproductions of more than one hundred previously published texts, including twenty-nine plays, seventeen poetry collections, twelve novels, six autobiographies, five collections of short biographical sketches, three biographies, three histories of organizations, three black histories, two anthologies, two sociological studies, a diary, and a book of etiquette. Each volume features an introduction written by a contemporary scholar that provides crucial biographical data on each author and the historical and critical context of her work. In some cases, little information on the authors was available outside of the fragments of biographical data contained in the original introduction or in the text itself. In these instances, editors have documented the libraries and research centers where they tried to find information, in the hope that subsequent scholars will continue the necessary search to find the "lost" clues to the women's stories in the rich stores of papers, letters, photographs, and other primary materials scattered throughout the country that have yet to be fully catalogued.

Many of the thrilling moments that occurred during the development of this series were the result of previously fragmented pieces of these women's histories suddenly coming together, such as Adele Alexander's uncovering of an old family photograph, picturing her own aunt with Addie Hunton, the author Alexander was researching. Claudia Tate's examination of Georgia Douglas Johnson's papers in the Moorland-Spingarn Research Center of Howard University resulted in the discovery of a wealth of previously unpublished work.

The slippery quality of race itself emerged during the construction of the series. One of the short novels originally intended for inclusion in the series had to be cut when the family of the author protested that the writer was not of African descent. Another case involved Louise Kennedy's sociological study *The Negro Peasant Turns Inward.* The fact that none of the available biographical material on Kennedy specifically mentioned race, combined with some coded criticism in a review in the *Crisis*, convinced editor Sheila Smith McCoy that Kennedy was probably white.

These women, taken together, begin to chart the true vitality, and complexity, of the literary tradition that African-American women have generated, using a wide variety of forms. They testify to the fact that the monumental works of Hurston, Larsen, and Fauset, for example, emerged out of a larger cultural context; they were not exceptions or aberrations. Indeed, their contributions to American literature and culture, as this series makes clear, were fundamental not only to the shaping of the African-American tradition but to the American tradition as well.

Henry Louis Gates, Jr.
Jennifer Burton

PUBLISHER'S NOTE

In the *African-American Women Writers, 1910-1940* series, G.K. Hall not only is making available previously neglected works that, in many cases, have been long out of print; we are also, whenever possible, publishing these works in facsimiles reprinted from their original editions including, when available, reproductions of original title pages, copyright pages, and photographs.

When it was not possible for us to reproduce a complete facsimile edition of a particular work (for example, if the original exists only as a handwritten draft or is too fragile to be reproduced), we have attempted to preserve the essence of the original by resetting the work exactly as it originally appeared. Therefore, any typographical errors, strikeouts, or other anomalies reflect our efforts to give the reader a true sense of the original work.

We trust that these facsimile and reprint editions, together with the new introductory essays, will be both useful and historically enlightening to scholars and students alike.

INTRODUCTION

BY JACQUELYN Y. MCLENDON

> In recognition of her meritorious community
> service, her deep concern for and participation
> in all activities advancing the status of women,
> her sincere effort and acceptance of responsibility
> to advance the brotherhood of man.
>
> —The Sojourner Truth Scroll

How strong must have been the desire of young Sarah Lee Brown to become the first black teacher in the Brooklyn school system, despite the disadvantages of poverty and race that she bore.[1] Worse, her own father advised her to join the ranks of domestic workers because he thought she would never be a teacher and therefore did not encourage her in her goal.[2] In addition to not giving Sarah moral support, her parents also often denied her the bare necessities. When Sarah asked her father for a new coat during her senior year in high school, he flatly refused. In the winter of that year she attended high school wearing "a man's old gray coat sweater" (Shockley, 356). The descriptions of these hardships also foretell the determination of this young black woman.

In the brief biographies she contributed to a volume entitled *Homespun Heroines* (1926), Sarah Lee Brown Fleming extols the virtues of two black women very much like herself, who devoted their lives to the social, economic, and political struggles of minorities and women. It is appropriate that she should have worked on such a book, for like the creative and extraordinary African-American women celebrated in the volume, Fleming did not "allow the confines of the hearth to limit [her] reasonable ambitions."[3] While married and the mother of two, she organized New Haven's Women's Civic League (1929), founded the Phillis Wheatley Home for Girls (1936), "a refuge for young colored girls who came to the city as strangers,"[4] and became the first black woman to be elected Connecticut "Mother of the Year" (1952). In addition to all of these activities, she wrote fiction and poetry, publishing a novel, *Hope's Highway*, in 1918, and a collection of poems, *Clouds and Sunshine*, in 1920.

As compelling as it is, the aforementioned information forms only a sketchy picture of Fleming's life. She was born on 10 January in Charleston, South Carolina, and grew up in Brooklyn, New York. In the sparse existing scholarship about Fleming, her year of birth is recorded as 1875; however, information provided by her husband at the time of her death establishes her year of birth as 1876.[5] Ironically, despite her own considerable achievements, little is known about Fleming before she married Richard Stedman Fleming and moved to New Haven, Connecticut. According to the entries on her husband in the 1927 and 1938–40 volumes of *Who's Who in Colored America*, the couple was married on 5 November 1902. Their children, Dorothy and Harold, were born in 1903 and 1906, respectively. When they moved to Connecticut, Richard Stedman Fleming became the first black dentist to practice in that state.[6]

In their day, both husband and wife would have been known as "race people." Sarah Fleming was an especially devoted worker and was cited before Congress in 1955 for her many community achievements and contributions. That year she also received the Sojourner Truth Scroll, an annual award sponsored by the National Association of Negro Business and Professional Women's Club. Perhaps she devoted so much of her time to helping others, especially less fortunate black women, because of her own early struggles, but, more importantly, she also firmly believed in racial uplift. In this regard, Fleming espoused the ideology of intellectuals of her day, and, indeed, participated in the uplift activities that were a preoccupation of the black women's club movement. In a letter to Mary Church Terrell, Fleming expressed her feeling that through the efforts of a kind of "talented tenth," people like Terrell

INTRODUCTION

herself, "much of the burden of the race would be lifted immeasurably."[7]

Fleming's writings are clearly inspired by this belief. *Hope's Highway*, her novel, is dedicated to a number of famous men "who have championed, and still champion, the higher aspirations of the black man."[8] The portraiture of Thomas Brinley, the book's black protagonist, is a composite of such men as Frederick Douglass, Booker T. Washington, and W. E. B. Du Bois, all of whom are listed on the dedication page. Fleming also acknowledges her use of material found in William H. Ferris's book *The African Abroad* because of its attention to great black men. Dedicated to Ferris's grandfather, Enoch Jefferson, *The African Abroad* may have even inspired the name of one of Fleming's black heroes, Enoch Vance, for Vance, like Ferris's grandfather, was a "faithful guardian of all interests intrusted to his care."[9] Ferris's work most certainly inspired a dominant theme in Fleming's book, that of the "educated leader" as "the Hope of the Race and the Hero in the Struggle for Negro Liberty" (Ferris, 363).

Hope's Highway begins in beautiful, idyllic Santa Maria, a fictional Southern plantation settlement, in the era of slavery. In the book's first few chapters, it tells of a slave, Enoch Vance, whose master, John Vance, freed and then educated him at a famous university so that he might lead his people out of poverty and ignorance. After Emancipation, Vance returns to Santa Maria and establishes a school for blacks, using a building and grounds left to him by his kind former master. Both the "Institute" and Vance are a great success until the rise of a group of antiblack politicians under the leadership of Joe Vardam. Through antiblack propoganda, wrongful imprisonment of blacks, and lynchings—under sanction of the law—Vardam's group destroys Vance's accomplishments, including the school. Vance dies of a broken heart. The story then focuses on a young black boy, Tom Brinley, alias Frank Hope, who is destined to be the new "leader," and a young white woman, Grace Ennery, who helps Tom by financing his Oxford education. Together Tom and Grace successfully integrate and bring peace and happiness to Santa Maria.

With the exception of several brief synopses of its plot, little else has been written about this novel. In addition to offering a fairly extensive recount of the story, Hugh Gloster briefly discusses several of the characters as well as speculates about Fleming's narrative intent. He concludes that the novel "has the usual overstatements of novels of its kind."[10] Another critic, Carl Milton Hughes, simply states that the book "piously resolved the race problem in religion."[11] While Hughes recognizes the significance of religious issues in the book, he ignores equally important issues of class. In *Hope's Highway*, the enemy of black people is "a class of poor whites," whose poverty is the "cause of their intense prejudice" (*Highway*, 48). The race problem is resolved through the efforts of aristocratic whites who, not only because of their religion, but also because of education and breeding, are able to overcome their prejudice and work with blacks who have not sunk to the level of the "idle class of Negroes" (*Highway*, 31).

In other words, religion is not separate from, but is conflated with class and race. Aristocratic whites like Grace, her family, and her friends are Christians, or at least are able to exhibit Christianlike behavior. The lower white element like Joe Vardam and his antiblack cohort Tilton are neither Christian nor Christian-like. The concept of religion for blacks, however, is articulated through the more complicated doctrine of the Noble Savage, conveyed early in the text by Enoch Vance, who, as his mother felt from the time of his birth, was "destined to be a Moses to his people" (*Highway*, 17). Later, it is Tom Brinley, a fifteen-year-old boy, "bare-footed, with clothes covered with patches" (*Highway*, 30), who is determined to follow in Vance's footsteps, a determination that Grace Ennery immediately recognizes: "O black boy,—with your look of exultation on your face,—surely some day you will be great with your wonderful determination." Tom has, she says, a "Divine" look that will make people "forget the hue of [his] skin!" (*Highway*, 30). While Tom and Enoch are extraordinary men, the Noble Savage leitmotif is conveyed through the essentially moral nature, indeed, the innate goodness, of all the significant black characters.

Both Hughes and Gloster accurately identify Fleming's desire to glorify black leaders, and Hughes includes *Hope's Highway* in a category of literature that lends itself to protest and reform. Yet part of the book's interest also lies in its being a historical

romance, one in which Fleming explores, like other authors of
the genre, "the effects of socio-historic events on humanity."[12]
True, the narrative only hints at the horrors inflicted on slaves
while rendering more explicitly the benevolence of their masters.
It also moves quickly from slavery to its aftermath, very much
like the narratives of Fleming's predecessors Pauline Hopkins
(*Contending Forces*) and, to a lesser degree, Frances Harper (*Iola
Leroy*).[13] However, Fleming's strategies coincide with her narrative intent: to illuminate the heroic deeds of extraordinary black
men, both enslaved and free.[14] Ultimately, Fleming attempts to
right a wrong that Ferris describes as "the Negro's peculiar weakness," which is that "he does not reverence his great men and
women, he does not appreciate the scholars and thinkers of his
race" (Ferris, 417). Ironically, it is perhaps this very wrong that
has rendered obscure Fleming's own life and work.

At the outset of *Hope's Highway* it might appear that Fleming
reverences great white men above black. Indeed, some aspects of
the initial chapters are reminiscent of plantation-tradition literature. The opening chapters on slavery describe John Vance as a
master so benevolent that his "name was held in reverence by
every Negro in and around Santa Maria" (*Highway*, 16) and
slaves prayed to become his property. The narrative also offers
numerous descriptions of his slaves' loyalty, such as how they
would sit in their cabin doors on moonlit nights singing the songs
he loved—"Lord, I'd rather go to Glory . . . than to leave this master kind" (*Highway*, 16), or a song that conveys an image of
mammy "crooning lullabies . . . full of rest and hope" (*Highway*,
13). The text also tells us that after Emancipation, "a great many
of the Blacks . . . remained with their owners" (*Highway*, 14).
Finally, when Vance is dead, "[black] men and women wept like
babies, as from their cabins they saw the body of their dearest
friend borne to its final resting-place" (*Highway*, 18).

Fortunately, Fleming also articulates the more usual cruelty of
slaveholders, such as the near-fatal beating of a slave woman by
Joe Vardam's father. For committing this vile act he is killed by a
slave, but his hatred of blacks and his disrespect of women are
passed on to his son. Vardam carries on his father's legacy with a
vengeance; he not only "held a bitter hatred for [blacks]," but also

beat, perhaps even killed, his own wife and abused his son (*Highway*, 60). Characterizations like this function to show that Southern race relations were no better during Reconstruction than during slavery. Thus Fleming subverts the traditional idealized picture of the South as it inheres in plantation literature. Further, Vardam's abusive treatment of his wife identifies a politics of oppression outside the boundaries of race through which Fleming introduces a feminist discourse that she more fully articulates in later chapters.

The world Fleming creates is primarily a world of men, but a female character, Grace Ennery, stands at the center of the novel. She is the granddaughter of Phillip Ennery, who had been a friend of John Vance and was himself a benevolent slaveholder. From an early age Grace develops an interest in and deep sympathy for blacks by listening to tales of her grandfather's kindness. Grace's position as a white heroine of a "black" story is an unusual narrative choice for a black writer of this time. The conventional heroine of early black fiction is the mulatto, often, in part, to elicit the sympathy and understanding of a sometimes hostile white audience. Fleming's heroine is not a mulatto, and there are no phenotypically white or racially indeterminate characters, nor a hint of miscegenation in the entire novel. The characters' physical descriptions are brief and racially coded to clearly distinguish blacks from whites. This enables Fleming to textually and contextually critique the prevailing myths concerning black and white behavior without authorial didacticism. The absence of racially indeterminate characters also eliminates the possibility of attributing to white blood any display of talent or any progress made by blacks. Fleming thus emphasizes that blacks' socioeconomic problems are "a matter of condition plus color" (*Highway*, 48–49).

Why, then, does Fleming, with her strong commitment to asserting blacks' humanity and subjectivity, make her heroine a white woman with "fluffy golden hair and large blue eyes" (*Highway*, 27)? I would argue, based on evidence in the text and also on Fleming's extraliterary views, that she is, in this instance, attempting verisimilitude. Here again she probably draws on Ferris's book, which states that with only a few exceptions, the emancipated slave "hardly owned the brogans on his feet" (Ferris,

326). None of the blacks in the novel have very much money over and above meager earnings or savings, except when they attract the patronage of benevolent whites, as do Vance and Brinley. Since Fleming needs a character who has money enough to pay for Tom's Oxford education, in reality she needs someone white. Yet, if she felt constrained to make Tom's benefactor white, she certainly felt no compunction to make that benefactor male. Thus a woman becomes one of the principal protagonists of *Hope's Highway*.

Grace Ennery's whiteness does not disrupt the complex relation Fleming's text bears to other black texts. Rather, Grace descends from a line of women characters in both white and black fiction who concern themselves with the moral and/or financial well-being of blacks. Harriet Beecher Stowe's *Uncle Tom's Cabin* (1852) apparently influenced *Hope's Highway*, as it did a number of other black writings. Even without the specific references to Stowe's novel (*Highway*, 24, 35), it would not be difficult to recognize the pious, tenderhearted Little Eva—in physical as well as moral demeanor—in the characterization of Grace. Grace's golden hair and blue eyes are religiously as much as racially coded signs, suggesting, along with her symbolic name, her angelic qualities. She is also reminiscent of Georgiana in William Wells Brown's *Clotel* (1853). This white character possesses the piety, honesty, and sensitivity that even her minister father lacks. Brown gives a white woman an uncommon understanding of the black psyche in order to express his own views about oppression and freedom without alienating his audience. Likewise, Grace understands the "Souls of Black Folks" (*Highway*, 39) when most other white characters in the book do not even believe blacks have souls.

Finally and perhaps most importantly, Fleming's choice of character reflects her optimistic view, of which the book's title is also emblematic, that the races can and will come together in mutual understanding and respect. Yet, it isn't only optimism or naïveté that motivates Fleming's construction of a "positive concept of history"[15]; it is also her belief in the ability of blacks, if given the same opportunities as whites, to achieve equality. Fleming protests white supremacist and segregationist ideology by creating a text in which a black character and a white character share the status of hero. Fleming "espouses a union of 'the best of both races' together forging a new culture deriving from equality," to borrow from Jane Campbell's argument with regard to Harper's *Iola Leroy* (Campbell, 31).

This strategy not only defines the polemical aims of the text but also challenges literary convention. As Hazel Carby points out, "In conventional terms, if an elite was to be the subject of fiction, black characters would have to remain on the periphery as servants."[16] This is certainly not the case in Fleming's novel, as evidenced by the characterizations of both Enoch Vance and Tom Brinley. Education, not skin color, enables black characters to move from the periphery to share subject position with elite whites in *Hope's Highway*. Thus, Fleming destabilizes the "disguise of whiteness," or passing, as a prerequisite for novels that attempt representation of race relations (Carby, xxxviii–ix).

When Joe Vardam falsely accuses Tom Brinley of stealing and sends him off to a chain gang, Tom's mother, Mandy, leaves Santa Maria and moves to New York. She happens to get a job as a laundress with a family who are friendly with the Grants, the people with whom Grace lives. Meanwhile, on the chain gang Tom meets Uncle Abbott, a wise old black man who could have been a leader "had he been given the chance" (*Highway*, 87). Uncle Abbott helps Tom escape, providing him with the names of people whose assistance eventually leads him to New York. Once there, through a series of coincidences, he finds his mother and Grace. In fact, Tom's fortuitous rescue of Grace from a fire is the single event that advances the remainder of the plot.

Although the narration is melodramatic, even maudlin, as it nears its end, this melodrama coincides with the book's romantic sensibility. An allusion to the mythological Psyche early on also signals Fleming's commitment to romance, as does a fantastical setting in which pious attitudes and heroic deeds flourish and magical resolutions take place: "Beautiful Santa Maria, land of the gods that nestles beneath wondrously blue skies [and] lies upon a luxurious carpet of green" (*Highway*, 11). In the beginning chapters of the book, Santa Maria is described as a "place where slavery was of a higher order" (*Highway*, 12), and by the end of the novel even negrophobes like the Grants, whose four-year-old child previously sang songs about "niggers," have been converted and live in harmony with blacks. Continuing the work of Enoch Vance with the help of aristocratic whites like Grace and her husband, Fred Trower, Tom Brinley "had turned his people's steps away from the rough road of ignorance into the happy highway of hope" (*Highway*, 156).

Yet, for all its magical resolutions and fantastic events, the novel's romantic sensibility is disturbed by a tension resulting from Fleming's political aims. For example, she includes a lynching that seems to have no connection to the plot other than possibly reinforcing the viciousness of some white people. The person who is lynched is neither named nor linked to any of the other characters, and the lynching itself excites the particular notice of no one except Grace. The novel's status as a historical romance justifies Fleming's inclusion of the lynching, despite its disruptive narrative effects. *Hope's Highway*'s publication follows close on the heels of the 1917 Silent Protest Parade down New York City's Fifth Avenue, a demonstration that protested the lynching of some 3,000 blacks since Emancipation. Still, the tension this scene creates stems from its structural placement in the narrative and from its use as a segue into a protracted discussion of black history between Grace and an old friend of her father.

Fleming also gives inordinate space to a farmers' conference, solely for the purpose, it seems, of praising "the farming experiences of these illiterate [black] country folk" (*Highway*, 82). The meeting is conducted as a kind of testimonial of farm experiences. It includes testimonies about blacks' "ingenious" methods of farming, about a black man who had risen out of slavery to become rich from farming, and about a black woman who had supported five children by growing cotton. The primary point seems to be to show "what Dame Nature has taught [black people]" (*Highway*, 81).

Although the attention given black women is not disruptive in the same way as the aforementioned events, these narrative moments also fall within the realm of realism as against romance. Just as Fleming uses the cult of the Noble Savage, in part, to advance the notion that blacks can rise "intellectually and financially" despite obstacles (*Highway*, 47), she also uses the cult of domesticity to advance a different political agenda. Black women in *Hope's Highway*, then, are not sacrificed to Fleming's other aims. For example, Mandy Brinley, Tom's mother, protests the inadequacies of the justice system. While she recognizes that there is a "criminal element" among black people, she also realizes that it thrives because "[T]he laws of the South had become so lax in the matter of offenses perpetrated by Blacks against Blacks that it was useless to complain" (*Highway*, 31). The text also describes an old woman, Nanna, who cooks for a well-to-do white family as one "who stood for the highest aims of the blacks,—with which race she was identified." Nanna says she's not "ashamed of [her] daily occupation," but would not like to see "all [her] people laboring in this field. They must scatter themselves in all avenues of work, in order to become a well-rounded, well-developed people" (*Highway*, 64).

Nanna's speech not only reaffirms pride of race and self, but it also fulfills another goal: as elsewhere in the book, it engages the controversy that accompanied Enoch Vance's establishment of the Institute for Negroes, a school quite possibly modeled after the Tuskegee Institute, though not entirely influenced by a Washingtonian aesthetic. Fleming places the objections to blacks' higher education solely in the mouths of whites, represented by Joe Vardam, who says, "We don't want any Niggers reading Latin and Greek. . . . Soon they'll be wantin' to call on us and be askin' to marry our daughters" (*Highway*, 20-21). Nanna's words are representative of the wisdom of the "leader," Enoch, and reiterate a belief that "a people just emerging from slavery could need nothing more than the rudiments of education" (*Highway*, 19), but also that gradually they should be given the same opportunities for higher education that were given whites. Without belittling Booker T. Washington's achievements, Fleming's character rejects his politics of compromise and his exclusive emphasis on industrial education for blacks.

While it is a white woman who occupies the position of heroine in the novel, it is the black women characters who demonstrate "the greatest potential of the women's movement" because they are "confronted by both a woman question and a race problem."[17] The discourse of racial uplift is appropriated here by what

Campbell calls "seemingly innocuous gatherings of women" (Campbell, 33), but these gathered women are, in fact, conveyors of politically charged messages that address issues of social change. Grace, on the other hand, is part of the romantic world fabricated by Fleming in which equality of the races is the right and only moral order.

Romance also accounts for several chapters of the book that contain Tom's various escapades in Europe. Fleming uses this opportunity to address "the question that his people were pressing . . . 'The admittance of the Negro into the State Militia'" (*Highway*, 143). Again, the year of the book's publication is germane to Fleming's focus on the issue of blacks in the military, for it follows the recent end of the war and a second well-publicized parade up Fifth Avenue of over a thousand black veterans. While Fleming focuses less on action in the romantic fashion, the rapidity with which she has Tom visit France, impress the French, join the army, and climb the ladder of rank is properly romantic: "[A]s commander of a regiment, he led a successful charge upon the enemy" (*Highway*, 151), and then in record time "Commander Brinley's fame . . . resounded through France, and England" (*Highway*, 152).

These tensions create in the text what Ann duCille calls the "unreal estate," defined as "a fictive realm of the fantastic and coincidental, not the farfetched or the fanciful or 'magic realism.'"[18] DuCille goes on to say that it is "an ideologically charged space created by drawing together a variety of discursive fields—including the 'real' and the 'romantic'. . . —usually for decidedly political purposes (duCille, 18). In *Hope's Highway*, then, the elements that stand in opposition—the real and the romantic—actually work together coherently within the text's own framework. They combine as part of the formal workings of the text, functioning to advance both its plot and its politics.

The feminist strain in *Hope's Highway* begins with the book's protesting violence against women and includes a reinterpretation of black domesticity. Another significant woman's issue inscribed in the text in several ways is the value of mothers. Grace Ennery is a "Poor Little Rich Girl" because although she has "every luxury," she is "bereft of that richest of blessings, a fond mother"

(*Highway*, 25). Fleming makes clear that even a "devoted" father could "never [fill] that void" caused by a mother's early death (*Highway*, 26). It is also noteworthy that Grace's father is absent at crucial moments in her life. After her mother's death, Grace was "dependent upon strangers" (*Highway*, 22), and just as Grace is developing into womanhood, her father, for his health's sake, prepares to take a trip around the world. He says to Grace, "I dislike to leave you at this time, when I know you should have me with you; but I must bow to my physician's command" (*Highway*, 27). Once again Grace must make her home with other relatives and friends.

Yet the absence of a mother does not equate with powerlessness in *Hope's Highway*.[19] Fleming revises historically affirmed roles for women by making Grace an artist and an activist and by asserting a woman's right to a career even while married. Unlike many novels by and about women wherein marriages take place at the end as a kind of narrative solution to women's problems, Grace marries well before *Hope's Highway* ends. Perhaps Grace's husband Trower's statement that "A woman is better able to express herself . . . after she marries" (*Highway*, 69) is a much more radical statement than one might think. Certainly Grace, very much like Fleming herself, continues to blossom as an artist after she marries and has a child.

Feminism is encoded in the text in compelling and at times even radical ways. Fleming makes Joe Vardam's father pay with his own life for beating a slave woman; the author also protests Vardam's physical abuse of his wife, addresses the issue of women's voting rights, and assigns to domestic women the cultural authority to speak on issues of political significance. If it seems as though black feminism does not quite achieve textual primacy, it is because of the concessions Fleming makes—a white heroine, peripheral black women characters—in her attention to the book's larger, controlling framework.

That Fleming used her writings to express, among other things, her political views is no less true with regard to her second book, a collection of poetry entitled *Clouds and Sunshine*. Dedicated to her children, the book is divided into three parts: the first seems to bear the name of the volume, although what could be the section's title is ambiguously placed; it contains poems on general topics of love, friendship, trust, patriotism, and religion. Most of these poems in some way embody sentiment associated with clouds or sunshine. The second and third sections—"Dialect Poems" and "Race Poems"—deal with racial themes.

While Fleming's poetry is not included in any of the major anthologies of or about the period in which she wrote, she, like other women and men writers at the time, addressed a wide range of social and racial problems. The difference between Fleming and her contemporaries, especially the women, lies not in subject matter, but in expression. In her anthology *Shadowed Dreams: Women's Poetry of the Harlem Renaissance* (1989), Maureen Honey includes poetry published from 1918 through 1931. In her introduction she argues, rightly, that much of the poetry produced by black women poets of this era has been misperceived as "raceless" and imitative when, in fact, it is "distinguished by subversive perception of the world and the use of subterfuge as a creative strategy."[20] Conversely, Fleming lyricizes an at times painfully blatant rhetoric of social critique.

As to imitation, the collection is so eclectic that it is difficult to pinpoint a particular tradition within which Fleming writes. The one consistent aspect of the poetry is that, with the exception of "The Black Man's Plea" and "Pictures," it is all heavily rhymed. At times Fleming sacrifices sense for rhyme, as in a poem entitled "Mammy": "Teeth so pearly, eyes so true, / Make you think of heav'n so blue, / That's Mammy."[21] The idea that Mammy's eyes are "so true" they remind one of heaven is lost to the emphasis on the rhymed couplet ending in "true" and "blue," thereby more readily conjuring an image of eye color. Since blue eyes would be entirely inappropriate for a woman described as "black of face," a comic image replaces the serious one I believe Fleming intended.

In addition to consistent and predictable patterns of rhyme, Fleming's poetry has a kind of structural sameness, perhaps because she was simply more concerned with content than with form. The one poem that demonstrates an attempt at structural innovation is "Pictures." Its stanzaic pattern unfolds like a series of snapshots, captioned "Slavery," "War," "Freedom," "Lynching," "Discrimination," and "Future," all of which provide a historic and panoramic view of race relations. The poem ends with the same optimistic vision as Fleming's novel, pressing the same integrationist ideology:

> My final picture is this one,
> 'Tis not with master, whip in hand,
> But it is Black and White, alike,
> Holding aloft the stars and stripes.
> They've buried far beneath the sod
> Grim prejudice and all lynch laws,
> And all in one united band,
> Proclaim the freedom of the land. (*Clouds*, 50–51)

In its entirety, "Pictures" is a poetic formulation of almost every theme in *Hope's Highway*.

The poems that cause the most consternation are the ones that perpetuate negative stereotypes or signal Fleming's own internalization of dominant standards of beauty, despite her assertions of race and self-pride. Unlike her novel, these poems demonstrate that Fleming clearly had some difficulty in "identify[ing] with the issues and interests of poor and uneducated black women," as Mary Helen Washington argues about some of Fleming's contemporaries who were equally committed to a politics of uplift (Washington, xlvii). A poem in the "Race" section, "Night Song," subtitled "Negro Lullaby," actually first appeared in *Hope's Highway*. In the novel, it is the song the slaves sing for the pleasure of their kind master, John Vance. What saves it from plantation-tradition condescension, however, is that the children Mammy comforts are not her master's but her own. This is quite unlike the aforementioned poem "Mammy," in which the children are racially indeterminate, with names like Jane and Sister.

In "Radiant Woman," the black mother who is objectified in the poem is beautiful only because of an inner Christian glow that outshines her "plain and homely," even "ugly features"; despite "its blackness," her face is "radiant as the sun." The speaker entreats others to "'Look you beyond the body, / Divinity you'll see!'" (*Clouds*, 40–41) The persona of the speaker attests to the distance between the author and the woman. The speaker, with whom the author identifies, has "pedigree behind her" and does not include herself in the "not very lofty" race of the black mother (*Clouds*, 40). This poem bespeaks the ideology of uplift, and therefore by its very nature creates a chasm between the speaker and the object of her exhortation on Christian love.

Fleming's inclusion of an entire section of dialect poems may have been a tribute to Paul Laurence Dunbar. Since Fleming herself wrote music, it also indicates her own interest in the lyrical possibilities of the vernacular. At the same time, in a poem like "De Tango Lesson" she seems to celebrate what has often been called the natural proclivity of blacks for song and dance:

> Watch Ephraim's pace,
> Now ain't dat grace?
> Lor' help me, dese darkies
>   is jus' eatin' up de place! (*Clouds*, 28)

While the poem is marred to some extent by the reference to "darkies" and, again, by Fleming's tenacious devotion to rhyme, an ambivalent ending calls into question, possibly even destabilizes, the prevailing myth regarding blacks' natural rhythm. After the exuberant descriptions of dance and "divine" music, the last stanza is curiously sobering:

> Here, clear de flo',
> Sam, ope' de do'.
> We ain't gwine to dance
>   dis tango any mo.' (*Clouds*, 29)

The abrupt end to the merriment not only disrupts the poem's prevailing imagery, but also foreshadows the seriousness of what is to come in the last section.

Interestingly, there are only two dialect poems in the "Race" section, and these are quite serious in tone. Lofty language and lofty subjects predominate. Even some of the topics of poems in the first section seem trivial compared to these, which portray "the deeper life" of black people (*Clouds*, 35). Like the single poem "Pictures," the controlling framework of this section is history.

Fleming moves from the era of slavery and descriptions of the "wounds" left by "chains of bondage" (*Clouds*, 35) to Emancipation and its aftermath of hope for black people. The implication of the change in focus is clear. As James Weldon Johnson would write a few years later, "It is now realized both by poets and by their public that as an instrument for poetry the dialect has only two main stops, humor and pathos."[22] Fleming's goal was to achieve dignity for her people. The concerns of the race were serious and needed to be presented seriously if ever African Americans' hopes were to be realized—that discrimination and racial strife could indeed be "pictures of the past" (*Clouds*, 50). Fleming saw her duty to blacks as similar to that of the poet in "An Exhortation" who is called upon to

> Sing them a wondrous story
> This burdened race of men,
> Paint it with all the glory that
> Can come forth from your pen.
> Set it to tuneful melody,
> As ever man did hear,
> So that a race benighted
> Will sing with heartiest cheer. (*Clouds*, 47)

Whatever she lacks in poetic skill, she makes up for in sincerity and conviction.

Sarah Fleming died on 5 January 1963, having lived her life fully. She was a wife, a mother, an activist, and, above all, an artist. Besides these two published works, Fleming wrote songs, skits, and musicals, among other works, that are not published. She took correspondence courses in creative writing and attended numerous lectures at Yale because "she felt her writing would be better . . . if she were able to improve her mind" (Shockley, 357). Yet, in the space marked "Occupation" on her death certificate stands the single word "Housewife." While this is one of the oldest and noblest duties of woman, and while from what we know of Fleming she would not have been ashamed of her "daily occupation," the lone word does not do justice to the life she lived. But then how could one fit in that tiny space all that she was?

INTRODUCTION

NOTES

[1]"Yesterday in Negro History," *Jet* (30 April 1964): 11.

[2]The most extensive biographical material on Fleming is contained in Ann Allen Shockley, *Afro-American Women Writers, 1746–1933: An Anthology and Critical Guide* (Boston: G.K. Hall, 1988), 356; hereafter cited in text.

[3]See Hallie Q. Brown, ed., *Homespun Heroines and Other Women of Distinction* (New York: Oxford University Press, 1988), 170.

[4]"A Tribute to Mrs. Sarah Lee Fleming," *Congressional Record—House*, 27 April 1955, 5186. Also see "Yesterday in Negro History," *Jet* (30 April 1964): 11, and "Wrecker's Crowbar Ended 20-Year Dream for Phillis Wheatley Home for Girls," *New Haven Register*, 6 March 1955, 22.

[5]Certificate of Death, Connecticut State Department of Health, Middletown, Connecticut. Both Shockley's *Afro-American Women Writers, 1746–1933* and *The Harlem Renaissance and Beyond*, edited by Lorraine Roses and Ruth Elizabeth Randolph (Boston: G.K. Hall, 1990) give Fleming's year of birth as 1875. Shockley states that Fleming died five days before her eighty-seventh birthday; since she died 5 January 1963, the 1875 date is inaccurate. Shockley also gives Fleming's father's name as Samuel, but the death certificate lists it as James.

[6]Joseph J. Boris, ed., *Who's Who in Colored America: A Biographical Dictionary of Notable Living Persons of Negro Descent in America*, vol. 1 (New York: Christian E. Burckel, 1927), 478.

[7]Letter to Mary Church Terrell, dated 9 March 1943, Manuscript Division, Library of Congress.

[8]See the dedication page of *Hope's Highway: A Novel* by Sarah Lee Brown Fleming (New York: Neale Publishing Company, 1918); hereafter cited in text as *Highway*. Page numbers given in these citations refer to the original edition, a facsimile of which is reproduced in the present volume.

[9]See the dedication page of William H. Ferris, *The African Abroad*, vol. 1 (New Haven, Conn.: Tuttle, Morehouse and Taylor Press, 1913); hereafter cited in text as Ferris.

[10]Hugh Gloster, *Negro Voices in American Fiction* (Chapel Hill: University of North Carolina Press, 1948), 97–98.

[11]Carl Milton Hughes, *The Negro Novelist, 1940–1950* (New York: Citadel Press, 1953), 36.

[12]Jane Campbell, *Mythic black Fiction: The Transformation of History* (Knoxville: University of Tennessee Press, 1986), 17; hereafter cited in text. In the introduction of her book Campbell also discusses the

critical debate regarding the paucity of black historical fiction before the 1960s. Campbell names Arna Bontemps, Frances Harper, and Pauline Hopkins as the exceptions to those who "eschewed the remote past entirely" (xiv). She does state, however, that more historical works by women will probably emerge as a result of the ongoing recovery of women's fiction.

[13]Campbell argues that Hopkins's and Harper's texts "reveal a preoccupation with the after-effects of slavery without devoting a great deal of space to depicting slavery" (Campbell, 31).

[14]Barbara Christian, in "Somebody Forgot to Tell Somebody Something," from *Reading black, Reading Feminist: A Critical Anthology*, ed. Henry Louis Gates, Jr. (New York: Meridian, 1990), discusses the three historical versions of slavery as defined by Margaret Walker, one of which is the African-American version that "tend[s] to focus on the lives of extraordinary slaves, almost always men" (334).

[15]Campbell discusses this tendency with regard to Frances Harper. See Campbell, 31.

[16]See Hazel Carby, Introduction to *The Magazine Novels of Pauline Hopkins* (New York: Oxford University Press, 1988), xxxviii; hereafter cited in text.

[17]See Mary Helen Washington, Introduction to *A Voice from the South* (New York: Oxford University Press, 1988), xlv; hereafter cited in text.

[18]Ann duCille, *The Coupling Convention: Sex, Text, and Tradition in Black Women's Fiction* (New York: Oxford University Press, 1993), 18; hereafter cited in text.

[19]For a more extensive discussion, see Marianne Hirsch, *The Mother/Daughter Plot: Narratives, Psychoanalysis, Feminism* (Bloomington: Indiana University Press, 1989), 44.

[20]Maureen Honey, *Shadowed Dreams: Women's Poetry of the Harlem Renaissance* (New Brunswick, N.J.: Rutgers University Press, 1989), 3. Honey discusses various critical reappraisals of women's poetry of the period.

[21]Sarah Lee Brown Fleming, *Clouds and Sunshine* (1920; reprint, Freeport, N.Y.: Books for Libraries Press, 1971), 25; hereafter cited in text as *Clouds*. Page numbers given in these citations refer to the reprint edition, a facsimile of which is reproduced in the present volume.

[22]James Weldon Johnson, *The Book of American Negro Poetry* (New York: Harcourt, Brace & World, 1931), 4.

HOPE'S HIGHWAY
A Novel

HOPE'S HIGHWAY

A Novel

BY

SARAH LEE BROWN FLEMING

THE NEALE PUBLISHING COMPANY
440 FOURTH AVENUE, NEW YORK
MCMXVIII

TO

THE FOLLOWING LEADERS, LIVING AND DEAD, WHO
HAVE CHAMPIONED, AND STILL CHAMPION, THE
HIGHER ASPIRATIONS OF THE BLACK MAN

THIS BOOK IS DEDICATED

HON. FREDERICK DOUGLASS

HON. GEORGE T. DOWN-
ING

HON. ROBERT B. EL-
LIOTT

HON. RICHARD T.
GREENER

HON. WRIGHT CUNEY

HON. FRANK GRIMKE

HON. ARCHIBALD H.
GRIMKE

HON. JOHN M. LANGSTON

HON. EBENEZER D. BAS-
SETT

JUDGE JOSEPH LEE

DR. BOOKER T. WASHING-
TON

DR. W. E. BURGHARDT DU
BOIS

BISHOP A. WALTERS

[5]

TABLE OF CONTENTS

FOREWORD

I have gained much information regarding the achievements and political status of the black man in America, and beyond the seas, from "The African Abroad," by William H. Ferris, A. M.

S. L. B. F.

HOPE'S HIGHWAY

CHAPTER I

SANTA MARIA

BEAUTIFUL Santa Maria, land of the gods that nestles beneath wondrously blue skies, lies upon a luxurious carpet of green, on a prominence overlooking,—as did Psyche of the myths in her liquid mirror of old,—the limpid Bay of Joan.

In the seventeenth century wealthy Spaniards had come over here in large numbers from the Old World and, because of its seclusion, had chosen this heavenly spot for a home. Across the bay was to be seen another ideal place, Santa Barbara, where to-day only the ruins of a once most extensive cotton plantation remain to show the existence of former grandeur. Negro men and women may be seen working in the fields, which show a few patches of cultivation. Rickety cabins, scattered thickly here and there, tell the tale of the passing of the masters of this once thriving island and of the reign of the Blacks; for investigation will show that no white man lives there now.

11

12 HOPE'S HIGHWAY

In Santa Maria may also be seen ruins of an old monastery, built by the Spaniards in the seventeenth century. After the state became a part of the Union, and the Spaniards gradually dispersed, other settlers came to this secluded spot, which, until the Emancipation, was one of the most aristocratic plantation settlements of the whole South. And in those days cabin life of the better sort was a conspicuous feature of beautiful Santa Maria and of its neighbor, Santa Barbara. It seemed the purpose of the owners of the Blacks to have this the one place where slavery was of a higher order,—if degrees of serfdom be possible.

The approach to Santa Maria was very beautiful. Imagine a shell-road of great length and width, lined on either side with drooping willows,—moss-laden,—some interlocking, forming spacious arches, and others opening sufficiently at the top to let in the Southern sunlight in all its regal splendor. The effect was almost fairylike. And to add enchantment to the scene, one could for an instant imagine these drooping willows bowing, as it were, most hospitably to the traveler, as if ushering him on and on to the resplendent glories of Santa Maria.

In the days of its glory,—after the traveler had left the willows behind,—imposing residences might be seen as far as the eye could reach.

From the quarters, on summer nights, plantation melodies were wafted on balmy breezes, and, as one drew nearer, crooning lullabies, sung by dusky mothers, could be heard,—lullabies so full of rest and hope.

Honey, take yo' res, on yo' mamme's breas',
See dat light,—a-fadin' 'mong de pine trees in de wes',
Yes; de day is gone, night is comin' on,
Darksome night mus' come to us befo' another dawn.

Whippo'will is callin',—callin' to his mate;
Mockin'-bird is callin', too;
Pine trees is a-sighin', babies is a-cryin',
As de darksome night is passin' through.
Go to sleep, ma little baby, go to sleep;
Shut yo' weary eyelids, an' don' you weep;
Sleep an' take yo' res', on yo' mamme's breas',
Night can never harm you here.

Honey, don' you see, dat it's got to be:
Day an' night, yes, day an' night, till yo' spirit's free;
Den you'll quit ma breas' fur to go an' res'
Wid another who can keep you safe from harm de bes'.

Masters here were more or less kind to their slaves, and, consequently, their reputation for gentleness spread far and wide. At the slave market one might observe a striking evidence of this; for whenever a buyer from Santa Maria or Santa Barbara came along, every slave showed up at his best upon the auction block.

When the deathknell to slavery was sounded and Lincoln signed the great Emancipation

Proclamation,—which spelled Liberty for millions of slaves,—a great many of the Blacks in Santa Maria and Santa Barbara remained with their owners.

Of these slaveholders, John Vance,—regarded as one of the wealthiest in this realm,— freed and educated one of his loyal servitors, with the idea that, should the freedom that the bondmen craved come to them, he could impart to his people some of the essentials necessary for a recently emancipated race to understand. Thus, Enoch Vance, taking his master's name, attracted much attention by his application and brilliancy at a Western university and returned to his former owner at the announcement of Freedom. Fortunately, he arrived in Santa Maria a few months before his benefactor's death.

John Vance, because of the manumission of the Negroes, had lost some of his vast fortune, but in his great generosity, he left nearly half of what was left for the education of the Blacks, whom slavery had kept so long in ignorance.

Upon his deathbed he sent for his former slave.

"Go," said he to Enoch, "and upon the land I shall give you, at the entrance of this beautiful Santa Maria,—land that I love so well,— facing the drooping willows and the shell-road,

erect a school that shall be a guiding star to
your people, lost on the road of ignorance. Be
a leader to them,—be a Moses,—safely carrying them over the Red Sea to the Promised
Land!''

CHAPTER II

John Vance's name was held in reverence by
every Negro in and around Santa Maria. How
many Black men and women in slavery had
heard of this good man and prayed that some
day they might become his property! Often, on
moonlight nights, he would listen to the singing
of his slaves, as they sat in their cabin doors,
voicing the familiar plantation melodies,—the
effect of which was marvelous,—as it passed
from door to door on the balmy breezes. One
song that particularly pleased their master
was:

Lord, I'd rather go to Glory, Lord, I'd rather go to Glory,
Lord, I'd rather go to Glory, than to leave this master kind.

John Vance was in the habit of visiting his
slaves in their cabins, he would talk with them,
and thus he became a part of their lives. He
never had occasion to whip a slave, never kept
an overseer, neither did he ever have a runaway. When a slave became in any way ob-
stinate or unruly, the master would only have

16

to suggest in a kindly way, that perhaps the
bondman would like another master; and, almost invariably, he would get the result he
desired. He could count upon the fingers of one
hand,—out of a thousand or more slaves that he
owned,—the few cases he could not handle.

Being of a very sympathetic nature, he often
wanted to help many a one who yearned for an
education; for if there was any aristocrat in
the South who desired to change the existing
laws regarding educating slaves, John Vance
truly was one. As soon as freedom came, he
secured teachers for those of the adults that
desired to learn, while the children were compelled to spend a certain number of hours each
day in the schoolroom. Indeed, his was the first
institute for Blacks in the South, being the fore-
runner of the many organizations that were
established for this race by loyal Northern sup-
porters.

The young Negro lad, Enoch, whom John
Vance specially favored, was born upon the
Vance plantation, as was his mother. His
father had been bought by Vance from a neigh-
boring slaveholder,—who had lost heavily in
speculation. The father of Enoch had courted
and married Enoch's mother; and when the son
was born his mother felt that the boy was destined to be a Moses to his people.

Knowing how Enoch's mother yearned for an

education, and seeing the same desire manifested by the lad, John Vance hoped that he might be able to start him on the road of knowledge. He was fortunately able to do this, by giving the lad his freedom and sending him to that greatest of Western colleges, which has ever held and which still holds open the "Door of Hope" to all who would enter therein. Thus Enoch developed into a true leader of his people, for he was the first Negro qualified to teach the Blacks in the South after Emancipation.

When John Vance lay dead in the Big House, Negroes came from far and near to view the abode of this true lover of humanity. Many, too poor to buy flowers, wrought wreaths out of wild flowers and lay them at the entrance of the Big House. Children could be seen strewing flowers in the familiar spots and along the roads he frequented. Men and women wept like babies, as from their cabins they saw the body of their dearest friend borne to its final resting-place.

After the closing up of the Big House, the late owner's widowed sister, who had made her home with him, returned North to her husband's people. The division of his lands was made according to John Vance's dying wish, which gave his belongings to the ex-slaves that had served him faithfully. And these same

people, by their frugality, became the hope of
the South, while by their efforts great business
enterprises were launched,—enterprises that
to-day, together with the Institute, are the
pride of the Black South.

This institute was a haven for the Negro.
Located picturesquely at the entrance of Santa
Maria and overlooking the Bay of Joan, it
seemed almost a temple in a land of promise,
and, flocking to its doors, came from all parts
of the world, those eager to learn.

Enoch first made the curriculum cover those
things that his people most needed,—agricul-
ture and manual training; for he was aware
that a people just emerging from slavery could
need nothing more than the rudiments of education. As time advanced, however, other departments were added, and finally from the
Leader's school emerged men and women fitted
for every vocation in life.

The Leader was heralded far and wide for
his great achievements. Even abroad he was
talked of, and educators of distant lands visited
his institute, for the purpose of studying his
methods of instruction. Great men from different parts of the country either gave their support financially or otherwise to the Vance Institute, and from its example other schools
sprang up, heralding, as did their Alma Mater,
"Higher education for the Black man."

This system of enlightenment in the course of time became unpopular with a certain element in the South,—an element that crowded in after slavery from the mountainous districts to the west of Santa Maria, or that came in by immigration. And, as the slaveholding aristocracy passed out by death or migration, these people became leading figures, soon wielding the political ax that chopped down all things that were unfavorable to them,—among them, the political status of the Negro, whom they considered to be growing too powerful. Throughout the South, state after state disfranchised the Blacks and decreed against higher education for them. Thus, because of legislative interference, the great ambition of the Leader's life was blighted.

Joe Vardam, an enemy to the cause of the Blacks, worked his way forward politically, fighting with tooth and nail to have the whole educational curriculum changed, so far as higher education for Blacks was concerned.

Realizing that he was utterly powerless to contend with this powerful demagogue, the Leader was compelled to bend to his will and strike out from his course of study psychology, sociology, comparative literature, law, theology, mathematics, and the classics.

"We don't want any Niggers reading Latin and Greek," Joe Vardam would say. "Soon they'll be wantin' to call on us and be askin' to marry our daughters."

The Leader remembered that his former master had often been upbraided in the State Conventions by this fellow, and he remembered, too, that Vardam had once shaken his fist in John Vance's face, remarking:

"If I ever get a chance to deal a blow at these damned Blacks, I'll deal some blow; believe me!"

True to his oath he dealt a deadly blow, and the Leader, hurt to the soul,—having had all his fond hopes blighted, and being powerless to ask, in the name of the law, protection in the exercise of a right that he considered sacred,— died of a broken heart, in the very prime of his manhood, leaving to the world the memory of a well-spent life.

CHAPTER III

PHILLIP ENNERY, a boyhood chum of John Vance's, was one of the great plantation owners in the prosperous days of Santa Maria. Phillip had two sons, one of whom, Francis, at his mother's death, left the South, when still a young man, with his share of the Ennery fortune, and entered the brokerage business in New York City. In the course of time he met a beautiful young woman, of Boston's most exclusive circle, and married her. She did not live long after the birth of her daughter Grace, and Francis Ennery was left a widower in New York with a little daughter of five years to look after.

Grace's maternal grandmother, who lived in Boston, was an invalid, and her uncle John Ennery had never married; thus the dear little girl, for a time after her mother's death, was dependent upon strangers. This fact was a source of some worry to her grandmother, who realized that, unless she could arrange to have the child under her guidance,—even though she were disabled, that the little girl would be

22

brought up among paid attendants. This she felt would not be the best thing for a child so young. Thus a plan was adopted by which Grace could remain with her grandmother until she should be old enough to enter a boarding school. After a competent governess had been secured, Francis Ennery returned from the "hub" to New York, grieved that his happy home life should be thus shattered.

Grace's grandmother was of Puritan stock, and reverenced those ideals for which her forefathers, desiring to enjoy freedom in a new land, had braved the dangers of the ocean and the terrors of warlike tribes. This love for liberty was so early implanted in the child's mind that we find her eager to hear the great stories of struggle and sacrifice and privation, for freedom's sake,—stories that her grandmother took pride in telling her.

As she sat with her grandmother she learned of the historical interest associated with the many places in and around Boston; and when she went out for her daily walks, she beheld these spots and loved them because of their glorious associations.

"Granny," she would often say, "tell me of the Boston Tea Party."

Then her grandmother would weave one of the prettiest tales concerning the "Tax on Tea."

Much enthused was she when she was told
of the Battle of Bunker Hill, and how her great-
great-grandfather had died in defense of the
rights of the colonists and how her grandfather
defended the rights of the slaves, taking an active part in the working of the famous "Under-
ground Railroad." The story of how he helped
them escape from their cruel masters in the
South greatly interested her young mind.

Grace never grew weary of listening to the
sorrows of the Blacks, and ofttimes she would
say to Charlotte, her governess:

"Take me where I may see these people that
Grandpa helped to get away from their bad
masters. And, Charlotte, show me a man like
Uncle Tom who was so good to little Eva."

As Grace grew to womanhood, she never forgot these pictures that her grandmother painted
for her in such glowing colors. The Negro,
wherever she met him, felt the sympathetic
spirit for his sufferings that animated the girl.

The years flew rapidly by, and with them
Grace grew, of course. Francis Ennery often
came to see his daughter, who began to look
more and more like her dead mother each day.
At the suggestion of her grandmother, who was
gradually declining, the father decided to
send the child to a select boarding-school, as
she was now twelve years of age. The day
Grace bade her dear grandmother good-by was

a sad one for her. How she hated to leave this place, with all its dear associations; for it was her mother's birthplace, the storehouse of everything sacred in her child-mind. Then, too, she loved the implements of war,—relics of the family's bravery,—that had their places here and there around the house, from cellar to attic.

Her spirits were revived only when her grandmother told her that she was going to the same school from which her mother had been graduated. This, of course, pleased Grace in a way; but it did not prevent her crying herself to sleep for the first few nights after her entrance. However, the beauty of the scenery, her joy in her studies, the happiness of her teachers, and the spirited life of the school soon revived her youthful spirits.

Thus passed Grace Ennery's years from girlhood to womanhood, surrounded by every luxury; for she was a rich girl, yet poor, too, in that she was bereft of that richest of blessings, a fond mother, to whom she might now and again unburden herself,—one whom she might kiss and fondle with the abandon of a spoilt child. So, after all, Grace Ennery might be called a "Poor Little Rich Girl." Think of the loneliness that came to her young life at times! Think of the yearnings! "She had a father," you say. Yes, she did, and a devoted one, too; but he never filled that void, or satisfied an instinct that lay hidden within her soul. And because of her warmth of feeling and her passionate yearnings, it was a wonder that the suppression of her longing did not make her sad and pensive, and thus embitter her youthful existence. Grace, however, possessed an indomitable will, coupled with a courageous heart, which kept her from ever wincing. Hence there bloomed into womanhood, under the faithful guidance of the teachers of Saint Agnes school at Lynhurst, a girl who developed the most beautiful character,—noble, strong, and modest.

After her graduation, Grace was sent abroad to study art,—for which she had formed a decided talent,—chaperoned by one of her instructors, who also desired to make further studies in the same field. Miss Arnold, who was very much attached to Grace, made a pleasant traveling companion, and two delightful years were spent studying the old masters in the different countries of Europe.

One morning a most unexpected thing happened,—Grace received a cablegram announcing that her father had been advised by his physician to drop his business cares and responsibilities for the present and take a trip around the world, and that he wished to see her before sailing for the Orient, by way of the Mediterranean.

On Grace's receiving this news, Miss Arnold comforted her and assisted her in every possible way so that nothing might delay her departure. And Grace, after being placed in the care of good friends, was on her way to America.

She reached home just before her father sailed for Greece and Egypt. In one of his last talks with her he said:

"As I look upon your face, you so remind me of your dead mother, with your fluffy golden hair and large blue eyes. I pray that you may develop into the noble woman she was. Remember always, Grace, that you were her idol. I dislike to leave you at this time, when I know you should have me with you; but I must bow to my physician's command. You have an uncle in the South, in beautiful Santa Maria, where I was born. I hope upon my return from the East to gaze once more upon those moss-laden willows, under which I had my first boyish dreams.

"All alone in a great house he lives, upon a plantation where once your grandfather held numerous slaves. He writes that you must pay him a visit soon, when you will see one of nature's enchanting spots.

"I have made my home with the Grants for a number of years, and they have been very kind to me. If you do not return to your studies, make your home with them: I am sure

they will be very good to you. The property
and stocks left by your mother have been wisely
invested and yield a large income. This, with
other sums that I have placed in trust for you,
will make it possible for you to grant your
every wish while I am away. Deny yourself
nothing, for there is plenty for everything.''

The next day Mr. Ennery left with his valet.
Grace found herself pleasantly located in busy
New York with her father's friends the Grants.
After getting somewhat acquainted, she returned to her work in the world of art, where,
because of her undoubted talent, she became
quickly known. She found Mrs. Grant very
busy with her numberless social duties,—entertaining and being entertained to a degree.

After a few months had elapsed, Grace decided to visit her uncle in Santa Maria. Shortly
after her arrival, her uncle was called to Europe
on business, and she was left in control of the
place. She enjoyed the delights of the big
house, but felt very lonely. So, wishing to see
and learn a little more of the South, she took
quarters in a nearby hotel.

Because of a deep sympathy for the Blacks,
formed in her early years, it was her delight to
wander with a friend or two,—but oftener alone,
—in the neighborhoods where they were to be
found, there to study their humble lives.

CHAPTER IV

THE Leader of his people lay dead, and as the funeral cortège wound its way into the peaceful graveyard, to lay at rest all that remained of a once powerful man, one could hear from the scattered groups of spectators such expressions as these:

"Who'll take his place?" "We'll now go to de dogs, for de white folks will surely do us bad." "Dey done peck on him an' peck on him till dey done kill him."

One of the old women began to sing, and others took up the strain:

> De Lord done take our Moses,
> De Lord done take our Moses,
> De Lord done take our Moses,—
> Who we gwine to follow now?

Deep into the heart of Tom Brinley sank these expressions; and, although but a boy of fifteen years, he was much disturbed. He suddenly felt the weight of a people upon his shoulders, and an irresistible impulse seized him to answer these poor dependent people.

29

Imagine a little brown boy,—bare-footed, with clothes covered with patches,—attempting to quell the sobbing multitude that had lost all hope, because of the death of the Leader! However, obeying the impulse, Tom sprang among the group of sobbing women, and with wide-open eyes,—eyes that brimmed over with sympathy,—and with the assurance of a man, cried out:

"Don't be sad; don't cry! Look at me. I'll lead you,—*I'll* be your Moses."

"O black boy,—with that look of exultation on your face,—surely some day you will be great with your wonderful determination. You truly have been sent to earth for some purpose. In your life the Divine will shine with such glorious brightness, that men will forget the hue of your skin!" thought Grace, who was present.

Surprised for an instant by Tom's words, the mourning groups temporarily forgot their grief and looked at the boy. When one woman had recovered sufficiently, she said:

"Go 'long, boy! You done gone stark crazy, you is."

Then a group of the rowdy element, of which the South is full, and who had gathered for no other purpose than curiosity, jeered at Tom, and one of them tripped him up. He fell against an iron rail, hitting his head, then lay upon the ground in a swoon.

Some kind-hearted men picked him up and carried him to his home, which was not very far off. "What of his assailants?" you ask. This class compose the criminal element of the South. Many of the lynchings in that region are occasioned by the misdeeds of some one of this idle class of Negroes, who care little or nothing about leaders or rights. Then, too, the laws of the South had become so lax in the matter of offenses perpetrated by Blacks against Blacks that it was useless to complain.

Grace Ennery, who was a witness to all that had happened, followed the limp body of little Tom to his mother's cabin of two rooms.

Tom's mother was a quiet, sympathetic woman of about forty, with large, glowing eyes, and a slightly bent frame, which told of much drudgery.

"Tom truly has her eyes," thought Grace, as she looked upon the mother. When the men who carried Tom told of what had happened, her reply was:

"Tom's always bein' pecked on. Folks don' seem to understan' him."

Upon a clean but humble bed they placed the little lad. Grace Ennery assisted in bringing him to.

"I shall never forget his deep, soul-stirring eyes,—so full of purpose," she remarked to

friends afterward. "As he came out of his
swoon his first words were:

" 'All right, Hollow gang, you shall yet call
me "Leader." Mother, didn't you hear our
Leader say that when he was a little slave boy
he would call the other slave children around
him and tell them that he would some day be a
great man and the leader of his people, and even
they would not believe him?' "

"Yes," replied his mother, softly stroking
his forehead.

"And, Mother," he continued, "see what a
great man he became."

Grace Ennery listened to the little fellow
with much interest, and when the crowd had
somewhat disappeared, she asked the mother
if she could be of any further service.

"Lor' bless you, dear lady," she replied.
"Tom is given to dem fallin' out spells, whenever any one hits his head. When he use to
work wid' Mister Joe, he would ofttimes send
for me to ris' Tom out of dem spells, when he
done hit him fur somethin'."

"Will you have those boys punished who
willfully meddled with Tom?" asked Grace.

"Oh, Miss, you mus' be a stranger here?"

"Yes; I'm from the North."

"I thought so, ma'am. De white folks don'
bother 'bout our troubles lessen they can't
help it."

"My! That is a very discouraging condition of affairs."

"Well, ma'am, we are gettin' so used to trouble, dat we don' look for justice till we die, an' then come judgment day," was the resigned reply.

Grace bade Tom good-by, and slipping a bill into his mother's hand, said:

"I expect to leave for the North in a few days, but will see you before I go."

Tom's mother bowed her visitor out graciously. It was somewhat new to her to have a sympathetic caller from the opposite race.

The Blacks at this time, owing to the injustice of Vardam, were so crushed that any white person having any relations with them other than those of employer and employed was considered an enemy to the cause of white supremacy. "Down with the Blacks!" was the slogan of Vardam and his allies.

Grace, of course, did not know of the sentiment regarding the Blacks, and even though she was the only white woman present, in her girlish optimism she had not observed it. Hers was a Divine sympathy, impartial and uncolored.

But, after all, a man's ideals, aspirations, hopes, and longings are not controlled by the color of his skin. Does not a brown horse that has broken his leg feel the same pain that a white horse does,—does he not demand the same amount of attention, regardless of the color of his hide?

CHAPTER V

THE next day was Sunday, and after attending church, Grace had a strong desire to glance at the grave of the dead Leader. This desire had been interfered with on the previous day because of the accident to little Tom.

She had never seen the Leader, yet, even in the North, his fame had reached her ear and she had learned to respect him for his achievements among his people. His success was greatly appreciated by the North, and his advice had been sought by men of high as well as low degree.

Knowing all this, Grace was desirous of seeing the mound of dirt under which the body of this famed Negro rested. So she sauntered slowly to that spot on the grounds of the great school that he had established. She was not known, therefore was not interfered with. But one cross-looking white man, who, to Grace's mind, had the look of a man who might have been a cruel slaveholder (such as she had read about in ''Uncle Tom's Cabin''), stopped her as she entered the grounds.

35

Turning around, Grace saw a picturesque but not a very prepossessing-looking individual, —a tall, raw-boned, and sinewy individual of about fifty, with a wide-brimmed slouch hat, tilted on one side; a long coat, and trousers tucked in leather boots, who walked with a long, swinging stride and spoke with a slow Southern drawl. But if his figure and attire were striking, his face was not attractive. Grace found herself looking into a pair of fierce devilish black eyes that gleamed beneath shaggy eyebrows. Besides these eyes she saw a decidedly hooked nose, which surmounted a thin, cruel mouth, and a long jaw, which was covered with a beard of medium growth.

But if the face was evil and sinister in repose, it took on added malignity as the man smiled sardonically. Plainly, here was a man with executive and administrative ability, with power to dominate the ignorant masses; a man possessed of a selfish, cruel nature.

"Say, miss," he said, "ain't you 'fraid to be travelin' in these Nigger haunts?"

"No," answered Grace, somewhat indignant. "So far you have been my only annoyance."

"Is that so?" was his surly query. "I guess you don't know who I am."

"Perhaps I don't, and neither do I care to know who you are, even if you were the governor."

"Well, if you ever get into trouble with these Niggers, you needn't bother Joe Vardam," he retorted angrily, turning away.

Grace walked on and soon reached the Leader's grave. She had made no reply to Joe Vardam's last remark, neither had she looked back; but had kept on until she came to the spot that she was seeking. This she could not miss because of the profusion of flowers that covered it. She rested upon a stone coping and gazed upon the many-hued flowers that, in the sun's dancing rays, seemed to stir and send their mingled perfume up to Heaven.

While sitting there wondering about the people whom this worthy man represented, Grace was startled by a rustle of leaves behind her. It was the first of October, when nature clothed herself in gorgeous robes of crimson and gold, and even the ground was covered with a golden leafy carpet.

Her revery broken, she turned and saw Tom. As she looked up, he cried:

"Ain't de flowers pretty, missus? Look! de sun is comin' down to them."

And the boy stood there entranced by the wedding of the sun and the flowers.

"Tom, you loved your Leader?" asked Grace sympathetically.

"Yessum," answered Tom, still under the spell of the scene.

Grace continued:

"Did you go to his school?"

"Yessum," he replied again, still not taking his eyes away from the grave.

"He must have been a very wonderful man to impress you so strongly. I hope some day you will be as great and influential a man as he was."

"I will, ma'am, if Joe Vardam don't turn de hose on me as he did the Leader."

"Who is Joe Vardam?"

"Didn't you pass a man when you come in de school?"

"Yes, I remember that I did."

"Well, dat's de one, ma'am, who would kill us all up if he could. He's powerfully strong, missus."

"So he interfered with the progress of the school?"

"Yessum. Folks call him 'Goliath' here, and they is all 'fraid of him."

"I hope he may some day meet his David, Tom," retorted Grace with earnestness.

The chapel bell tolled two, and Grace arose to go, bidding Tom, who still was looking admiringly at the flowers, good-by. She told him that she would be leaving for her Northern home soon, but would see both him and his mother before she left.

Grace walked slowly to her hotel, thinking of the sorrows of this race.

"O black boy," thought she, "too sensitive were you made! You, too, shall have many sorrows, for my people do not believe in 'Souls of Black Folks.' "

The next day Grace, sitting at her window at the hotel, after supper, glancing over the daily papers, was startled by a heinous yell. Looking out, she saw four white men dragging a poor Negro to the park, which faced the hotel. On their trail a thousand whites followed, crying at the top of their voices:

"Lynch him! Lynch him!"

She had heard and read much of lynchings, but never thought she would witness such a barbarous scene, enacted by her own people. Yet, here was a poor fellow,—perhaps innocent of the crime with which he was charged,—being brutally killed, without being able to utter one single word in defense of himself.

Quickly they strung him up to a tree and, daubing his body with pitch, struck fire to him. In telling of the fiendish deed afterward, Grace said:

"The sight was too brutal for words. Soon the sizzling and crackling of the fire could be heard, and the smell of human flesh was stifling. I wanted to satisfy myself that real people were implicated in the deed, but as I looked upon the

upturned faces it seemed as if the spirit of
humanity had fled from that mob and that in
its stead a living devil was implanted. 'Oh!'
thought I, 'I cannot dwell another night among
these people.' So, in my excitement, I packed
my grip and went to the office to settle my bill.
After having done so, and while waiting for
transportation to the depot, I encountered the
same man whom I had met on the previous
day. He quickly recognized me and said with
a laugh:

" 'I am sure glad you are going, miss; for
we will certainly have to string up another
Nigger to-morrow.' Then he gave a fiendish
chuckle and passed on."

Grace never bore any hatred in her heart for
any one, but this man, Joe Vardam, had created
within her a most uncomfortable feeling.

A few moments after her encounter with him
she was whirled off to the depot. Reaching
there, she found that she had leisure on her
hands before her train was due. She wondered
just how to pass away the time. She wanted
to talk with a real sympathizer, or with one,
who, even if he were not a sympathizer, possessed a tinge of respect for his community and
had ideals. Looking around the partly filled
depot, she saw no promise in the faces of those
around her. Her eye was attracted toward the
door, and there she saw an immaculately

dressed man of middle age,—tall and symmetrical of frame,—with the air of a born aristocrat. He was ushered in by a black lad who seemed to be showing him every attention. After he had arranged for his baggage, the lad left him, courteously bowing.

"Surely," thought Grace, "this is a man I can talk to,—one from whom I may gain information regarding these parts that no one whom I have yet seen would willingly give me."

Before he had espied her, she arose, and as the bench upon which he sat had only one other occupant, she quickly sat there, waiting for an opportunity to speak.

The aristocrat, as soon as his eyes rested upon Grace, regarded her with deep interest.

"Pardon me," he said; "are you an Ennery?"

"Yes," she quietly replied, fearful lest he might discern her eagerness to talk.

"You came here, I suppose, to visit your ——" he paused.

"Uncle," Grace quickly replied.

"Oh, yes," said he; "then Francis was your father? We were boys together, and our parents were good friends."

Grace found herself drawing very near to the opportunity for which she longed,—to be able to glean the information she desired.

"How do you like the South?" asked her companion.

"Not at all," she answered. "I am going home sooner than I anticipated, because of the crime perpetrated before my eyes."

"Oh, the lynching, you mean. That has become a common occurrence in these parts, I regret to say."

"I regret to say," meant worlds to Grace. It made her feel that she had met a sympathizer.

CHAPTER VI

SANTA MARIA, PAST AND PRESENT

"I AM so glad to hear you talk thus," remarked Grace. "If it would not seem inquisitive, I wish you would tell me why the Blacks have so little protection in a country so unique in its Republican form of government. I have always loved my country, and even though I knew conditions were not so very good in the South, I did not understand it to be a condition that resulted from gross injustice on the part of my people towards a people powerless to protect themselves."

"My dear Miss Ennery, you are too conscientious in this matter, I fear. We all would like to see the millennium if we could but the world is not ready for it yet."

"We may not be ready for the millennium," interrupted Grace, "but we should at all times use our consciences. Right is right, sir. Oh, pardon me if I have been too bold. Of course you know that I am a Northerner, and while, for so young a woman, I may express myself in too frank terms regarding my attitude

43

toward your treatment of the Blacks here, yet I feel that I am justified because they are human beings and our brothers; and we are our brothers' keepers.''

Mr. Garrett assured Grace that she was justified in all she had said, and that her view was no different from that of the average Northerner. Yet even the Northerner, he went on, after residing in the South for a time, often became more bitter in his attitude toward the Blacks than were those that had always lived there.

Along came the train, and emerging from some inconspicuous corner, the black boy, who assisted Mr. Garrett some time before, came forward to be of further service to his employer. Mr. Garrett, speaking very kindly, bade him take Grace's luggage to the car and arrange her comfortably.

At parting with her recent acquaintance, Grace said:

''I thank you so much, sir, for your patience in answering my questions. I shall go away with a different impression than I would have had had I not met you.''

''You flatter me, Miss Ennery. I am the one who has been benefited. I would like to, at this moment,—if I had the power,—make such laws as would give every black man, woman, and child better protection. Since we have had this

pleasant little chat, and also since your father
and I are good friends,—also your uncle,—I
trust you may give me the privilege of hunting
you up on the train, and continuing this conversation, if it is agreeable to you.''

"I shall be delighted," replied Grace.

So, giving her one of his cards, the old aristocrat handed her over to his body-servant, who
courteously escorted her to her seat.

The car was well on its way to the North, and
Grace had settled herself quite comfortably,
when Mr. Garrett found his childhood chum's
daughter. Grace was much impressed with her
new-found friend, and waited, with profound
anticipation, to hear what of interest he had to
tell her.

Before delving into the all-important question, he told her that he was on his way to the
governor of the State to report on the recent
lynching, which was a great source of grief to
the committee of which he was a member. This
committee, he further stated, consisted of a
group of men, selected by the governor, who
met after such disturbances as lynchings and
riots, passed judgment upon them, and reported
their findings to the governor.

"Why can you not stop such riots before
they go as far as they did this afternoon?"

"A lynching-bee is often gotten up so suddenly that frequently in one hour it is both

planned and executed. When we are able to
jail the victim, we are more likely to protect his
body.''

"Please tell me," Grace asked, "how things
ever developed to this state of affairs, in this
beautiful settlement, where nature's artist has
painted so lavishly, the skies, the bay, and the
trees, and where everything is bathed in an
atmosphere of serenity.''

Settling himself comfortably and clearing his
throat so that he might be distinctly heard
above the rumbling of the train, Seward Garrett began:

"In 1870 the Negro was given the ballot in
this State. About that time a Negro was made
secretary of the State. A number of colored
men also went to Congress. Negro legislators
held regal sway in the capitol, with their ma-
hogany tables, Brussels carpets, and Dresden
china cuspidors. At the change of administra-
tion, in 1876, the Federal troops that protected
the rights of the Negro were withdrawn from
this State, and when other complications came
up between Republicans and Democrats, the
Southern Confederates took possession of the
State capitol by force. Then came the Ku-
klux Klans. They were oath-bound societies,
the members disguised with masks and armed
to the teeth. They rode at night, committed
depredations, and did their bloody work. They

intimidated Negro voters, drove them by force
from the polls, and suppressed the Negro leaders until eventually the constitutions of the
Southern States practically disfranchised the
race. But in spite of all these drawbacks, the
Negro rose intellectually and financially. Of
course you have heard of the Leader's school.''

''Yes, I have been on the grounds,'' interposed Grace.

''Well, then, you saw what, in spite of great
opposition, he accomplished. He was forced,
because of the interference of the Democrats
here,—who hold political sway, of course,—to
cut out all of the higher courses from the curriculum. This has been a great blow to the
Blacks, as nothing above the elementary grades
can be taught now.''

''Do you not think this very unfair, Mr. Garrett?''

''Well, I suppose you do; but down here
they do not think the Negro ready for the higher
stuff yet.''

''Well then, the politicians are supposed to
be the judges as to when the brain can accept
certain branches of information. If they are
able to determine this, then they know more
than all the seers ever knew. Mr. Garrett, few
human beings have ever desired anything along
intellectual lines unless they were ready for it.
'Tis sad to blight the higher bent of man, 'tis

cruel,—man must at all times, to develop the highest within him, be a free agent. Oh, 'tis all wrong, all wrong!''

"It may be, but time will tell. And remember, Miss Ennery, the worst enemies of the Blacks are not the descendants of their former owners, but a class of poor whites who have pushed in from the mountains, and who never knew of them, other than that they crowded them out of a livelihood, by having the monopoly of service. This condition, of course, kept them very poor, barely above starvation; hence this is the cause of their intense prejudice. These people prospered after Emancipation, and to-day are the life, politically and commercially, of the South. The Negro, it is true, was caught in a mesh that he is still untangling. It is evident that the only satisfactory solution will be for him to find his own way out."

"But how can he do this, without the protection that his country should offer?"

"I don't know, but he must do it some way, Miss Ennery. We Anglo-Saxons surely must have found an opportunity to wedge our way out of the conditions that we first faced generations ago."

"Yes, I know, Mr. Garrett; but these people have a far greater fight than our Anglo-Saxon ancestors had. Saddest of all are the distinct physical characteristics, so unlike ours, that make the problem a matter of condition plus color.''

Mr. Garrett, looking at his watch, found that he had nearly reached his destination. So getting up, he wished Miss Ennery a safe journey home, and asked her to come at some future time and visit his home in Santa Maria, where his wife and daughters would be most happy to welcome her.

After Grace had thanked her companion for his courtesy, and, too, for his extreme kindness in explaining matters so plainly as to racial conditions, they parted as the train rolled in to the capital of the State.

CHAPTER VII

DARKNESS had not yet completely taken possession of the landscape, and Grace sat admiring the Southern sunset,—with its wonderful golden hues,—as it fell upon the autumn foliage, making a most gorgeous display. The skies, so wondrously blue, made Grace wish for her palette and brushes.

"Nature is so generous," she thought; "depriving none of us,—no matter how humble,—of her grandeur!"

Looking away toward the west, she discerned mountains. "Those must be the mountains that Mr. Garrett referred to. There was the home of the 'poor whites,'—made poor by slavery. Surely there must be a law of retribution. In crushing the slave our own people were crushed, because an inferior element sprang up,—an element that would never have come into existence but for the importation of slaves."

After traveling a day and a night, Grace reached New York. Mr. and Mrs. Grant met her at the station. They were whirled quickly

50

home; and she, being quite fatigued, without saying very much of her trip, went directly to bed.

Before going to sleep she wondered what she could do to help the colored people; for she determined to do something for them.   Never having made a study of the sentiment of the North with regard to this race, and not knowing to what extent prejudice existed, she resolved to find out.   In a way she had been removed, nearly all her life, from the world at large, because of her mother's death.   In a select boarding-school one would hardly hear of the Negro and his condition, and similar problems, discussed to any extent.

Grace thought that she would try to find out the Grant family's opinion regarding the question that dominated her young mind.

This family consisted, beside Mr. and Mrs. Grant, of a girl of twelve, a boy of ten, and a baby girl of four.

"Aunt Grace," said Margaret, the oldest daughter, after dinner the next night, "we missed you so much.   We thought that the Niggers had stolen you; didn't we, Mother?"

"No, Margaret, they did not bother me in the least,—in fact, I enjoyed seeing them and talking with them."

"O Aunt Grace, what could you find interesting in these people?"

"A great deal, Margaret. I found them very much like ourselves in every way except color. And in the South, many who were pointed out to me as colored were really as white as you or I."

"They are wicked and bad and were made by the devil," chimed in Jack, who had left off his reading to listen.

While Mrs. Grant,—one of those mothers who experience difficulty in controling her children,—was trying to quiet Margaret and Jack (for she had quickly seen that their attitude was distasteful to Grace), Baby Elleen was singing:

> "Eeny, meeny, miney, mo!
> Catch a Nigger by the toe;
> If he hollers, let 'im go,
> Eeny, meeny, miney, mo!'

"No, children, you must not deride these poor people: their lot is so hard, and they need a helping hand," remarked Grace earnestly.

"O Aunt Grace," remarked Margaret, "I couldn't love a Nigger,—I couldn't."

"Then give them your sympathy," said Grace, rising.

Mr. Grant was not at home, so Grace did not have a chance to sound his views. However, the opportunity was offered the next evening at dinner.

As they sat chatting on various subjects, the

maid announced the fact that the same Nigger who called the other evening was at the door.

"Tell him I don't care to see him, and I don't want him to be ringing my front-door bell again or I'll have him arrested. Wanting me to offer a bill to introduce Niggers into the State militia! Absurd! Niggers with firearms! I'd sooner trust these emigrants that are pouring in upon our shores."

The maid left the room while Mr. Grant was expostulating, and soon Grace heard the front door close with a bang.

Mr. Grant had entered the political arena, while the Great War was on, to protect certain of his Wall Street interests. The war in Europe being over, this country was facing some complicated issues.

Emigration seemed to have reached a serious stage. After the European war, this country, in its generosity, opened its gates without any reservation. To this land came various classes of foreigners to avoid the responsibility that would devolve upon them of building new homes in Europe. Upon this country's investigating a number of plots to blow up various buildings, it was found that anarchists had come over in large numbers. So, in order to avoid the danger that might arise by permitting more of these anarchistic spirits to infest the country, a ban was placed upon emigration. This, of course, was not kindly accepted by many, yet it ultimately became a law.

Then the Negro wanted to serve his country, by admittance into the State militia, where he might be trained as a soldier. This did not meet the approval of many, who were opposed to Negroes' being armed.

These were the pressing questions of the time, and were being seriously discussed.

Mr. Grant, as Grace Ennery saw, was an enemy to her cause. And as such things dawn upon us when we wish to make use of them, she remembered that her father had told her some time ago that he was stopping with folks whom he knew years ago in the South. Now she could see why he spoke thus. She did not comment at all upon his last expression, but discerned in his countenance something that recalled Joe Vardam vividly to her mind.

"I wonder," she thought, but she would wonder no more. She wished to dismiss the dreadful thought from her mind, and said to herself: "No, it cannot be."

After chatting awhile with Mrs. Grant she retired for the night.

While arranging her hair for bed Grace resolved that she would use a portion of her income in behalf of the Blacks. Just how she would do so, she determined to leave to her maturer judgment.

Grace now became very busy, taking up her work in art, where she had left off. Because Mrs. Grant insisted, she went out occasionally to social functions. Her hostess was a social butterfly, flitting here and there, wherever pleasure could be found. She was happiest when being entertained and entertaining. This, —entertaining,—she was very capable of doing, because her husband provided liberally for her. She had no special aim either for herself or her children. She was continually on the go, and could never understand why Grace would not appreciate her opportunity to mingle in the highest society.

"Grace," she would often say, "you are wasting your youth by not seeing more of life."

"Do you think so, Mrs. Grant?" Grace would reply. "I feel as though I would like to accomplish something before I took up social duties, for I know from observation that I could never do much more than keep up with society, were I to enter it."

"That may be true to some extent; but at your age you should never talk so. With your money and opportunity, many a girl would consider herself blessed."

Then the maid would announce Mrs. De Allen or Count Van Silver, or Fanny de Forest, and away Mrs. Grant would glide bedecked in silks and diamonds, worn with dignity supreme upon a super-stately figure, crowned with a madonna-like face. Whereupon Grace would betake herself to her own apartment, unless requested by Mrs. Grant to stay and meet her distinguished guests. Then she would be agreeable, because she felt that she must.

CHAPTER VIII

THE LETTER THAT FAILED

In her art work Grace Ennery was by no means mediocre. She attracted attention on her return from abroad by a beautiful painting of two children entitled "Love." In the picture one of the children, a boy, climbs an apple-tree to bring down the last apple,—far out on a frail branch,—to the girl.

Frederick Trower, a patron of art, contributing generously to the cultivation of the fine arts in New York City, was attracted toward Grace, and during her previous stay in the city had called upon her frequently.

During the war Mr. Trower was called abroad to protect the interests of his father in Paris, and from time to time Grace would receive some word from him,—as she would from her father, who was at this time in Egypt. Not very long after her arrival home from the South, Grace found at her place at breakfast a letter postmarked "Paris." She hastily ate and returned to her room to read it. The portion that had the greatest weight with her read as follows:

57

I don't know what your attitude is toward the Negro, but
you may be interested in knowing that the French army has
enlisted many of these black men in the ranks, and the report
is that they make brave soldiers, going into the hottest of the
fray, without reserve or fear.

One herculean black was given a medal of honor a couple of
weeks ago, for his bravery in battle. His physique was magnificent,—tall, erect of stature, and well proportioned. He impressed one as he stood to receive his degree. The French people could not do enough for him. Imagine my attending a ban-
quet in his honor! The French seemed to have forgotten his
color, and spoke only of his valor and bravery.

After all, Grace, I feel that we Americans are too narrow in
our feelings. What difference does it make whether bravery is
garbed in black or white? It is deeper than the skin. It
reaches the soul, and the soul of the good is always white.

I know you have come in touch with these black people of
the South. Tell me your opinion as gained by your trip.

Grace, after reading this interesting letter
from Fred Trower, unconsciously wiped her
eyes, and held the missive to her lips.

"I have decided," she said half aloud. "I
have decided to act upon my convictions. The
light that I have desired has been given to me."

Immediately she sat down and wrote a letter
to Tom Brinley's mother, in care of the Institute, as she had failed to get Tom's address
in her excitement in leaving.

Now, in Santa Maria politics had control of
everything. Even the mails of colored people
were continually being tampered with.

It happened that the day Grace's letter
reached Santa Maria, Joe Vardam was loung-
ing around the post office as he usually did. As
his money was made more or less from political

graft, he often, when he had time on his hands, helped Billy, the postmaster, sort the mail. In coming across this letter marked "New York," and written in a legible hand to Tom Brinley's mother, Joe Vardam became curious.

He had always had a suspicious feeling regarding this fellow. He watched the development of his precocious mind with envy, as he feared he might attract attention, especially among those who were Negro sympathizers. Often he shook his fist at the boy and told him to keep scarce.

As soon as Joe Vardam discovered the letter he told Billy that he would deliver it. Briskly walking to his cottage, where he lived alone, and stealthily entering it, as if he feared even his own conscience, he lit a kerosene lamp and hastily read the following words:

MY DEAR MRS. BRINLEY:

I have been thinking of Tom ever since my return. I wanted so much to talk with you about him, but the dreadful lynching hastened my departure.

I want to educate Tom, and send him abroad if necessary. I want to help him develop the splendid nascent manhood which slumbers in his nature.

After reading this much, Joe Vardam chuckled.

"Ah, my dear woman, you will be baffled this time. You'll not get your wish, if I can balk it."

Joe Vardam was a politician of the lowest

type. There was nothing too degrading for
him to do in order to gain his ends.

It was whispered that he had beaten his poor
wife to death, and that he drove his son from
home, when the latter would not coöperate with
him in political wrongs. Where the younger
Vardam went no one knew.

It was also whispered that Joe Vardam's
father, a very cruel slaveholder, was killed by
one of his slaves, because he thrashed a woman
slave until she became unconscious. The slave
in turn thrashed him, and when Vardam's
father drew his pistol to shoot him, the slave
wrested it from his hand and shot the master.
Then the homicide gave himself up to the authorities to be dealt with as they saw fit.

Joe Vardam, whether because of the manner
of his father's death was seeking vengeance
or because of the natural cruelty that possessed
him, was relentless wherever a Negro was concerned. For some reason he held a bitter hatred
for the race.

After thinking over the letter during the
night, Joe Vardam determined to place Tom
Brinley where he would never attract attention. Day after day he walked the streets of
Santa Maria in search of his prey, wishing to
catch him away from his home and surround-
ings. Not many days had passed by when he
found his opportunity. Noticing that the

Leader's grave was bare, and not having enough
money to buy suitable flowers, Tom, after
school one day, told his mother that he was
going over to San Joan to gather wild flowers
for the Leader's grave. Just as he was about
to embark across the stream in a little row-
boat, which he found on the sands of Santa
Maria, he was seized by the collar by Vardam
and dragged back to the settlement.

"All right, you little rascal, you will hang
around stealin' boats and idlin' your time away,
—will you? I'll fix you. To the chain-gang
with you!"

When Tom Brinley's mother heard of her
child's arrest, she tried in every way to reach
the proper authorities, in order to speak a word
in behalf of her son. The way seemed barred,
for she was told that what Joe Vardam had
passed judgment upon could not be changed.
In her great grief she decided to leave Santa
Maria and seek the North, as she had now lost
all hope. She had saved a little money for
Tom's schooling. This she took. After closing up her home in which she had spent so many
happy days both with her husband and her boy,
—she took the boat for New York, where she
hoped to get something to do to try to forget
her great affliction. Her friends sympathized
with her and kept her in touch with all that was
transpiring in Santa Maria.

Her kindly, sympathetic face won for her a
good home with the de Forest family, who had
advertised for a good laundress.

One day Miss de Forest had a young people's
party, and among the invited guests were the
little Grants. Running around, as children
will, Elleen roamed into the kitchen, where she
came across Mandy Brinley, who was sobbing.
Soon the child had assembled all the other little
ones at the door to watch the sobbing woman.

At the Grants' supper-table that night the
children told of the colored woman's crying in
Miss de Forest's kitchen; at which Grace expressed great sympathy.

"Aunt Grace," said Margaret Grant, "her
son was stolen in the South by a cruel man and
put on the chain-gang."

"That is very sad," answered Grace. "Suppose Jack were to be taken from us suddenly,
without warning, and we were never to see him
again?"

"Oh, that would be awful!" chimed little
Elleen. "Is some one going to steal our Jack?"

"I'll shoot them," said the little fellow, by
way of defending himself.

CHAPTER IX

Days and weeks passed and still Grace received no reply to the letter she had sent. She could not determine what she was to do next. In the meantime she still worked at her art, expending her greatest efforts in the painting of a likeness of Tom Brinley (as nearly as was possible), a painting that she named "Purpose."

A member of the F. N. P. (Federation For Negro Protection,—a group of influential Whites and Blacks, formed for the protection of the rights of the black man in the North and the South), seeing the picture, asked that it be loaned for an exhibition that they were about to give. Grace gladly consented to this, and the picture was placed in the Gallery of Fine Arts.

Nanna, the old cook at the de Forests' house, by way of making it pleasant for Mandy Brinley, asked her to attend the exhibit with her. This Nanna was a woman who stood for the highest aims of the Blacks,—with which race she was identified. Often she would say,

63

"I'm a cook, an' I'm not ashamed of my daily occupation, for a good cook must take pride in her work; yet I would not see all my people laboring in this field. They must scatter themselves in all avenues of work, in order to become a well-rounded, well-developed people. I am always anxious to know what all my people are doing."

Hence her interest in the exhibit, which marked an anniversary of progress for her people.

The great armory where the exhibition was held was crowded,—the F. N. P. having also invited a number of speakers, both white and black, to talk in behalf of the Negro. The absorbing themes were, "The Negro In Office," "The Negro In Politics," and "The Negro In The Army."

How Mandy Brinley wished for her Tom; and in walking about after the great addresses, she, as if her prayer was answered, came face to face with a painted reproduction of her Tom.

"O my Jesus!" she cried, "Nanna, here's my boy,—here's my Tom!"

"Go on, Mandy; you've got your boy on your mind so you imagine everything is him."

Grace Ennery and Fred Trower were also present. They almost passed Tom Brinley's mother as she turned from the picture in great grief. Grace in her absorption in other exhib-

its did not see Mandy. But Fred Trower saw
her, and he remarked to himself that the wonderful eyes of the lad must have made her sad.

Nanna and Mandy returned quietly home,—
Mandy laden with sorrow. Grace and Fred,
after the interesting meeting, sauntered leisurely home. They talked of the speakers, especially the Negro speakers, who knew what their
people needed.

"I am sure Tom Brinley would do equally
as well as any of those speakers, were he given
the opportunity to develop himself," said
Grace. "It is so strange that I never received
any reply to my first letter to his mother,—
and my second was returned to me."

Fred replied:

"Grace, I am afraid you are taking matters
too seriously. Sometimes those whom we
would wish to be worthy are altogether unworthy."

"Not so with Tom; he has a strong will, and
I am quite sure that he, although young, has
determined to develop in the direction of his
natural taste and aptitude."

"Now, Grace, I begin to think that you never
intend to devote any of your time to me. Since
I have returned home, you have had this and
that to interfere with our pleasant little chats,
—such as we use to have."

"Forgive me, Fred, if I have appeared selfish since you have returned. It is not selfishness; it is really that my life is broader. Unexpected problems have come before me, and I am anxious to grapple with them.''

Whether Grace knew it or not, Fred Trower was in love with her, and had been so even before she went abroad to study art. Whenever the desire urged him to say something of his tenderness to her, her mind seemed always centered on something else, which made any declaration of love at that time quite inopportune.

When they had reached home, Fred asked Grace to give him an evening and to promise him for once not to speak of any of her pet hobbies, but to give up the entire time to him.

''It is a small favor, Fred,'' answered Grace. ''You may have your wish, of course.''

''All right, I shall see you to-morrow evening. And if Mrs. Grant has company, be prepared for a walk, as these evenings are very enticing in the open.''

''Very well. Good-night,'' said Grace, as she endeavored to disengage her arm.

Instead of freeing the arm immediately, however, Fred Trower pressed it gently and looked into her large blue eyes, which, with upturned gaze, met his. The look was like the meeting of two souls,—each read the heart of the other. Quickly Grace, as if she had committed a mis-

deed, went into the vestibule, remaining there
until the maid admitted her. The maid noticed
a flushed look upon Grace's face, as she thanked
the girl and ran swiftly to her own apartment.

Fred Trower stood for a moment as if glued
to the spot. Then, collecting himself, he turned
and hastened away.

Grace, when she reached her luxuriously appointed apartment,—consisting of bed-room,
private sitting-room, and bath,—yielded to an
irresistible impulse to run to the bay-window of
her sitting-room, which permitted her to see
a distance up the street. There she sat, hat
and coat on, watching pass on under the bright
electric lights the manly, erect form of the
man about whom was now the glamour of a
young girl's love. When he had passed out of
sight she slowly disrobed, and went to bed,—
thinking of many things that before this night
had never seriously entered her mind. To-night
Tom Brinley had no place in her young mind.
Hers was a dream of love, with Fred Trower
crowned king.

The next day seemed to two persons the long-
est day upon the calendar; and when the sun
was slowly sinking in the west, two hearts were
beating with gladness.

Grace was ready long before the maid announced Mr. Trower. Fred was prepared long
before he came. His father noticed the new

light in Fred's eye, as he closed the lid of his desk and hurried off, calling back:

"Good-night, Dad."

His father's look followed him to the door, and he questioned:

"Something on to-night, Fred?"

But his son was gone.

When the maid did announce the presence of Fred Trower in the parlors below, the fact had already been known to Grace some time. She was seated behind her curtain, on her window-seat, waiting,—in accordance with the demands of society,—to be told what she already knew.

Softly she stole downstairs,—so much more softly than was her custom,—and, with an air of coquettishness, sat opposite her lover. No word had yet been broken, when Fred, full of ardor, and not knowing how to free his pent-up feeling, rose and bent over her, saying:

"Grace, you know it all, do you not? Need I tell you how tenderly I love you? You do care for me some, do you not?"

Grace held her head back, and looking into Fred's eyes, replied softly:

"Yes, Fred; I think I do."

Then his head bent lower, and their lips met, after which Fred sat beside Grace, her hand in his and their heads together. Fred told her of his great love for her, how he hoped that it would be reciprocated; he also told her of his splendid prospects, and asked if she would consent to become his wife.

Grace answered:

"Not yet, Fred. I must do something of worth before I accept the very tender care that I know you are capable of giving me. Let me devote more time to my art before anything definite is decided."

"Why, Grace, you have done something! What more commendation can you wish than has been given to your pictures,—"Love" and "Purpose"?

"But that is just a beginning, Fred. Then there is Tom Brinley. Must I leave him? Should I not try to find him and help him?"

"Then, may I hope that you may tell me something definite as to our final plans when this little colored boy is found? As to your art, Grace, you can do even better work after you marry. A woman is better able to express herself, whatever her sphere in life, after she marries, because her life includes a broader scope. About the lad: my father wants me to look into some cotton interests in the South soon, and I can extend my trip, visit the Institute, and inquire about the boy."

"Dear Fred, you are so considerate, and I am so thankful that you will do this. I have a peculiar feeling concerning this boy, some inner prompting that urges me on.''

''Well, don't worry any more, Grace. Everything will come out satisfactorily. So you have really decided to educate this colored lad?''

''Yes, Fred; my desire is to give him an opportunity to serve his people.''

''I trust that he will prove himself worthy of your interest.''

''I am sure he will. By the way, Fred, I received a letter from my father, who is in Egypt now. He spoke very highly of you, and much of his friendship with your father. He says that his stay will be an extended one, as the Egyptian climate agrees with him better than any other that he has been in. He speaks in glowing terms of the scenery of the Nile, and has been captivated by the grandeur of Egypt's monuments. He has seen the pyramids, the Memnonion Colossi, the Temple of the kings at Luxor, and the vast Hypostile Hall at Karnak. He also writes that my uncle has joined him, having attended to his business affairs in Europe. How glad I shall be when he returns!''

''When I write and tell him of our plans, I shall insist upon his returning for our wedding, which I trust will be in the near future.''

They finished the evening with happy talk

on topics that would naturally be of interest to engaged couples.

Fred Trower was overjoyed. The fact that Grace Ennery had truly agreed to share her future with him made him show his delight without any reserve. He was a handsome fellow of about twenty-eight,—nearly seven years Grace's senior,—yet there was something quite boyish in his air to-night, Grace thought as she looked at him admiringly: his complexion was so clear, his soft brown eyes so full of sympathy. Eyes and hair were so exactly of the same shade that one wondered how nature could match in humanity her colors so harmoniously.

Any one gazing at the man at Grace Ennery's side,—with his hair slightly ruffled, looking admiringly into the girl's face,—would at once recognize and be amused at the boyishness portrayed in his manner, and would consider him not so bad for an only child, humored and petted as only children usually are.

Time flew by so rapidly that it quite surprised the young lovers when they heard the hall clock strike eleven.

When Frederick Trower rose to go, he looked so pleadingly at Grace that she could not resist going over to him and throwing her golden head upon his breast and permitting him to caress it with all the fondness that his manly nature could display. Then he left her with her promise, that a date of marriage would be set as soon as Tom Brinley's future had been arranged for.

A few weeks later Fred Trower left for the South.

CHAPTER X

AFTER reaching Richmond and arranging business matters, in accordance with his father's suggestions, Fred took the train for further South.

The South was not new to him. He had been there a number of times, as his father had various financial interests in different sections of the country; yet he had never been there bent on the mission he had now undertaken,—the search of a poor little brown lad.

All along the road he studied the people, —especially at the depots, which seemed a veritable "hang-out."

"I wonder," thought he, "if these people will ever carve out their own destiny? Judging from these laggards, who seem utterly dependent, one would say not."

These were merely passing thoughts, and Fred did not allow them to worry him seriously. He felt that Grace had enough philanthropy for them both.

After an extremely hot and dusty trip, he reached Santa Maria. He took a carriage, and

73

having reached the hotel, went directly to his apartments, as he felt very dusty and tired.

In the morning, which was an extremely warm one, he awoke early. After breakfast he walked around town and was attracted by the beauty of the place. Roses were in bloom and nature had everywhere a glad, smiling look.

Quite an inquisitive gaze was bestowed upon Fred when he asked at the hotel:

"What is the best time to visit the Vance Institute?"

The clerk quickly replied:

"We don't know much about them Niggers; they stay over on that side, and we stay on this. Nobody much bothers about them. They tell me that the school is going to the dogs. You came down to look 'em over, I suppose."

"Yes," said Fred, not wishing to prolong the conversation with this somewhat contrary individual.

He passed out of the hotel door and went down the steps, walking off somewhat slowly down the street. He had not gone very far when a somewhat repulsive looking man, tall, middle-aged, and carelessly attired, overtook him.

"Lookin' us folks behind the sun over, I suppose?" he ventured.

"Well, somewhat," replied Fred. "You have a pretty nice town here."

"Yes, but things have gone somewhat to the dogs, on account of these lazy darkies down this way. Can't make 'em work unless you beat 'em. There's that fine school that fool Vance put up for 'em, an' they don't even have enough attendin' to keep the doors open."

"Are you acquainted around these parts?" asked Fred,—for he thought that he might get the information he desired from this man.

"Yes I know everybody in and aroun' Santa Maria,—white an' black."

"Then you probably know something of a Tom Brinley?"

"That little black thief an' idler? Of course I do. What do you want with him?"

"I am trying to find him for a friend of mine."

"Well, you won't come across him 'round these parts. He was sent to the chain-gang in the backwoods for idlin' and stealin'."

Fred did not seem as shocked as one might think at hearing this, for all along the road, he had seen the Negro's idleness. And since theft follows such a weakness, it seemed just natural.

"What did your friend wish with this little black devil?" asked Vardam, for it was he.

"She thought that she saw some good traits in him and wished to develop them."

"What Nigger has any but bad traits?   A

woman too! Good Lord! My good man, keep
her away from Niggers, or she and you will
regret it some day.''

Fred never found the Institute, in fact he had
no desire to hunt for it, after talking with this
man. He lit a cigar, and puffing it complacently, slowly returned to his hotel.

On the veranda he stopped to watch the
Southern sunset. Slowly and slowly Old Sol
sank to the western horizon, and when almost
all had disappeared, the rest dropped suddenly
out of sight. As Fred Trower witnessed this
sudden dropping, he thought of how Grace's
fond hopes had vanished like a dream.

He said to himself:

''It's all tomfoolery her coming down here
and getting interested in a trifling black lad,
who was not worth a rap. Anyhow, I have done
my part. I wish Grace would not get so
wrapped up in these good-for-nothing people.''

After staying around another day, Fred
started for home. He ran into a college chum,
who was traveling in the interest of an agricultural society, and he persuaded Fred to attend
this Farmers' Conference with him.

Jerry Dill did not mention the fact that this
conference concerned the Blacks as well as the
Whites; for if he did, I do not think Fred
Trower would have troubled to go.

He was not a narrow man,—he tried to view a subject from all sides before arriving at a conclusion; yet he failed to see anything other than absurdity in his errand to Santa Maria. When his friend, Jerry Dill, found that Fred had some time to spare, he persuaded him to attend the Farmers' Conference,—not that Fred Trower was one bit interested in farms or farmers nor did he have any special desire to hang around the South; but the air was somewhat balmy and his love for nature met its response in everything in bloom. So Fred told Jerry that if it were not for the tugging at his heartstrings that drew him home, he would like to remain in the sunny South for an indefinite time.

The friends alighted at a little town, about seventy miles from Richmond, called Hollis, and found a pleasant little boarding-place. After Jerry had made all necessary arrangements for the following day he and Fred roamed around the village for a little fresh air.

As they wandered off the main road, they came to a settlement of cabins, behind which were richly cultivated tracts of land. At the doors of the cabins groups of blacks were congregated.

"This settlement," said Jerry, "is one of the most progressive in the South. The Negroes are very energetic, and this section produces larger crops for its size than any other known settlement.''

''How do you account for this unusual progress here?'' asked Fred.

''Well, I suppose the main thing is that these people get better treatment,—that is, there are fairer laws and a better spirit on the part of the authorities here than elsewhere. It's only a matter of human treatment after all, Fred,— the better you treat a horse, the more he will love you and the more devotedly he will serve you.''

Even with what Jerry had said, Fred was still reticent in talking of his prime mission in the South. He did not state his own opinions but simply allowed Jerry to air his ideas, and now and then he would inject a question or two of his own.

''Who attends these conferences, and what good is derived from them?'' asked Fred.

Jerry replied:

''Well, as I said, a mutual feeling exists between the races down here on matters of mutual concern. All attend the conferences and one gleans information from the other's experiences. That is why this agricultural society sent me down here. They selected this place because they feel that where race hatred is least bitter more good will be developed. As you know, hatred, be it of races or individuals, retards progress. This is why I feel that the South is behind the North,—because it spends a good bit of its time and valuable energy trying to crush the blacks politically and otherwise.''

Fred still did not comment but listened attentively. Soon the two retraced their steps, and until a late hour sat upon the boarding-house veranda and smoked: Jerry dreaming of the excellent reports he would be able to take back to the Agricultural Society, and Fred dreaming of Grace, the girl of his heart, and of her disappointment when she should hear the bad news of her would-be protégé, Tom Brinley.

After the two, amid circles of smoke, had dreamed to their heart's content, they went contentedly to bed.

CHAPTER XI

THE FARMERS' CONFERENCE

THE next morning when Fred Trower awoke
he wondered what impressions he would gain
before the day was over. His disappointment
had been so great that he had not written to
Grace since his arrival in Santa Maria. Rising
late, he missed Jerry, who had left a note stating that he would be found at Town Hall, where
the conference would be held. Fred ate his
breakfast leisurely, then wrote a note to Grace,
stating that he would tell her everything as
soon as he should reach home, which would be
in a few days, and that at this writing he was
attending, with a college chum, a farmers' conference at the place mentioned. After mailing
his letter, he walked leisurely toward the Town
Hall.

As Fred approached the Hall he saw the most
interesting sight he ever witnessed in his life.
Every kind of vehicle that could be mentioned
stood outside the place and, upon looking in
different directions, he still saw more coming.
Some,—the better situated financially,—came

80

in autos and others came on horseback. Occasionally, the father, mother, and child were carried on one poor horse. Then others came in wagons, in shays, on mules, and in ox-carts.

The colored women were dressed in every bright color one could think of. Some wore hats, with style and without style. Red bandannas seemed to have the day among them. The styles effected by the men were various. Vests were in as many colors as were the women's dresses. And Prince Alberts were almost in as great evidence among the men as red bandannas were among the women. Fred did not know whether he was attending a farmers' conference or a Baptist convention.

When he entered the hall, he saw a goodly number, both white and colored, seated. Many seemed to be conferring, one with the other, and, to his surprise, the atmosphere was most genial. Jerry Dill had seen his friend enter and take his place amid the crowd of farmers, and knowing that Fred would enjoy the sight better from the platform, he sent down for him.

"Some style!" said Fred to Jerry as he was escorted to a seat.

"Yes, old pal; but just you wait and see what they know. Just listen and hear what Dame Nature has taught them. What they know from that sincere teacher would surprise some of our fair lads and lassies in high school."

The meeting was called to order by the moderator. As Fred looked around him, he was surprised to see the class of men that had come to listen to the farming experiences of these illiterate country folk.

The meeting lagged somewhat at first, as one would naturally expect. The innocent country folk had to be aroused, just as the little seeds and plants need to be drawn out of the earth by the sun.

At length one large colored woman arose and told how she was supporting her five children by growing cotton.

" 'Tis de swelles' cotton dat grows anywheres aroun'!" she cried enthusiastically.

She told of how the land had been at first a hollow pond, of how her boys had filled it in and fertilized it, and of her great success.

Black speakers and white were interspersed, but Fred found the Negroes far more interesting, because of their ingenious ways of doing things.

He listened with enthusiasm to a colored farmer whose clothes were less gaudy than any of the rest. The moderator introduced him as the richest Negro for one hundred miles around.

The speaker arose, and in an unassuming manner spoke of his rise from poverty. He told of his father's and mother's being slaves, and of his being taken away from them when he was quite young, and of their being sold and going away, and of his never seeing them again. He told of how he would watch the soil and study the growth of things, and of his great success in raising cotton, and how to-day he shipped more cotton of the finer grade than any other farmer in the South.

Fred whispered to Jerry:

"It's wonderful, Jerry, I must admit."

Another burly black man told of the planting of the legumes and of the plowing of the roots under the soil, enriching it with nitrogen, which produced the element necessary for the growth of a number of plants and vegetables that he called by name. He also spoke of the rotation of the crops, thus preventing taking from the soil the same mineral matter year after year. He said that planting different crops every year kept the soil rich for the next crop.

After a few more talks all present filed out to the grounds for dinner.

"A picnic in the biggest sense!" thought Fred.

Jerry took Fred around among the farmers, showing him the cooked materials, all of which had been raised by them.

Fred remarked afterward to his Northern friends,

"Everything looked too good to be true. As

for fried chicken,—many of the colored farmers' wives had it over the French chefs of the Waldorf-Astoria.''

The next morning Fred thanked his friend Jerry and left Hollis for the North, feeling that his trip South had not been such a failure after all.

CHAPTER XII

TOM BRINLEY IN CHAINS

Tom Brinley, grieved to his soul, lay upon a hay bed, in a broken-down little hut,—a figure to move any one to pity. Chained to him was an old man,—Uncle Abbott,—seventy years of age, whom the cruel overseer always used to break in young prisoners. Uncle Abbott took mightily to the boy and urged him not to show much strength, as it would go hard with him. Thus, Tom reserved his energy as directed by his adviser, and well it was that he did, for he was to stand in great need of it later on.

Vardam and Tilton were in league with other political leaders to keep down those Negroes who manifested any degree of independence. These, they branded as "dangerous characters." It was their usual plan to trump up some charge of misdemeanor and then send them to the chain-gang in order to keep the others in the community in submission.

Tilton incarcerated Uncle Abbott because he pastored a set of his people who were always in fear of their employers. Uncle Abbott

85

taught them never to stand in fear of any one but God. These people were so ignorant that they continued to serve their old master in the same capacity as they had in slavery, not really knowing that they had ever been freed. This knowledge was kept from them by their white employers, and it was agreed among these employers to keep them ever thus. Tilton was a political demagogue in these quarters, and pronounced judgment against any one that tried to enlighten the people otherwise.

Thus, Uncle Abbott posed as merely the preacher for these people; but secretly he had a knowledge of their ignorance, and, with an assumption of shrewdness, effected to teach them humility. When not spied upon, however, he told them of their freedom,—of Lincoln and the Emancipation, teaching them, too, their rights. The effect was soon seen. A number of the Blacks left Holding for other climes.

When Tilton heard of this, he questioned Uncle Abbott, who replied:

"Yes, I told my people of their freedom; and now my work is done. You may do whatever you wish with me. It was my mission, and now it has been fulfilled."

"To the chain-gang with you!" cried Tilton. "Lynching is too good. I must put you where you can be tortured and tormented,—you deceiving beast!"

Thus Uncle Abbott was sent to the chain-gang, and had been there two years when Tom Brinley came. Two favors he asked of his in-carcerators,—to be able to take his worn and torn Bible, and a little grip that held a few pieces of worn clothing. His wish was granted.

When Uncle Abbott went to Holding to preach, he had taken with him money, which was hidden between the worn covers of his Bible, for he did not know when he might be forced to leave. Thus he could depend upon this money which he had saved to get away with, should the opportunity be offered to him. When he found that he did not have the chance to escape, as he had anticipated, he resignedly faced the situation. He had almost forgotten that he had this money, when Tom came upon the scene.

After he had heard Tom's sad story from the boy's own lips, and had discerned his aptitude and indomitable spirit,—which would mean much to his people,—he determined to help the lad make his escape.

Uncle Abbott was not a man of much learn-ing, but he was possessed of tact and a native shrewdness which mastered any emergency. He truly would have made a leader, had he been given the chance. In Tom he saw true worth and appreciated it, and all his mental energy was spent in planning for this boy an escape from a life of torture.

"Here is worth," he would say to himself as he would watch the boy asleep. "It must not let its life-blood be sapped in these backwoods. My people are crying for men, and more men. I have had my day,—I have done my Master's bidding. But, Tom, the power of God is greater than the devil. I shall pray for your freedom, and it will surely come."

In his satchel he had a little tool-kit, which no one knew he had there. No one ever watched him, as he had never attempted to make his escape, or the escape of any one else, before, even though he had brought his tools for this purpose. He had heard of this place, and knew that many an innocent man had perished in these chains. And in his profound grief he did not forget that he might have a chance to be of service,—even in the chain-gang.

CHAPTER XIII

UNCLE ABBOTT awoke Tom one night, and told him what he intended doing. Tom pleaded with the old man not to jeopardize his own life by trying to assist him. Uncle Abbott told him not to fear, that he knew the road well and that he felt that Divine guidance would clear the way of any obstacles that might arise. As their hut was located right on the road of escape, he told Tom to follow the road, until he came to Toddsville, where he knew a good Christian family, that would shield him from harm.

"Go to them," he said, "and tell them that I sent you, and they will drive you over to Cherry, where you can board a train for Maryland. After reaching there, buy some decent clothes, and go directly to New York,—where you can pass under another name,—and seek work."

Tom listened attentively to Uncle Abbott; he knew that the guards were situated at the other end of the cabins, for they did not consider it

89

necessary to be very watchful of Uncle Abbott, as he never attempted to escape. And even if Tom did, they knew he could not get very far with Uncle Abbott chained to him. No one ever suspected that the old man had in his possession means by which he could undo his chains if he so desired.

In the moonlight Uncle Abbott released Tom's chains, and put into the lad's pocket all the dry bread he could gather. After he had given him the money from between the covers of the Bible and had wished him God-speed, he bade him to go quickly and quietly. This was too much for Tom. He appreciated his friend's great kindness, but he felt that to take the money, which Uncle Abbott might some day need, would be an imposition. He told the old man that he would rather take his chance at finding something to do, and working his way on to New York, than to take that which he might some day need.

But the old man replied:

"No, I will not consider you out of danger until you have crossed the Mason and Dixon line. Prejudice to-day, my boy, is very rank down here, and if you are caught anywhere in the South, I know that they will place you where there will never be any hope. So take this money, and travel as fast as you can to your destination. You will for quite some time be only a few hours in advance of your pursuers, who will be on your heels as soon as they have discovered that you have escaped. Take these tools and bury them somewhere along the road. Be off, my boy, be off!''

Tom bade the old man good-by, saying:

''I shall never forget you as long as I shall live, Uncle Abbott, and if I should get safely to the North, without interference, I will work hard to acquire the power to some day destroy this place that keeps in chains such good people as you.''

Then Tom went out stealthily into the night, in the direction that Uncle Abbott pointed out. When he had gone some distance from the cabin, he heard steps and to his dismay came face to face with one of the guards. As quick as a flash he saw his fate.

''To hesitate means death,'' thought he. So before the guard had really recognized him, Tom made a dive, similar to a flying tackle in foot-ball, and threw him. The lad seemed for the moment to be endowed with supernatural strength. Before the guard could rise or get him fully in his grasp, Tom dealt him a blow across the head with the tool he had not yet disposed of, and fled.

After that unexpected encounter, Tom in his excitement was on the alert every moment, but he met no one else. He reached Toddsville, bedraggled and dusty, about nine o'clock the following morning. Seeing some men on their way to the fields, he asked them to direct him to Uncle Abbott's friends. This they did without questioning the poor boy, who presented a veritable picture of distress.

When Tom found the people and had told them his sad story and the story of Uncle Abbott, their grief knew no bounds.

Tom had just finished his tale of woe when the folks were startled by loud voices outside. Their suspicion was immediately aroused, so they hid Tom in a load of hay. Then Aunt Fanny and Uncle Joe went on with their work, planning that as soon as they had got rid of these trailers they would get Tom to Cherry as quickly as possible.

Sure enough the voices belonged to those that were hunting for Tom. They yelled to Aunt Fanny, asking her if she had seen a little Nigger come along that way.

"Yes," returned Aunt Fanny "a long time ago, an' he look so queer, I knowed he wus up tu mischief. He asked me where Rootville was, an' I showed him, an' off he trotted."

Now, Rootville was in the opposite direction to Cherry, and after looking through her cabin the men hurried in the direction Aunt Fanny had indicated. When the trailers were out of sight, she put Tom on horseback and directed him to Cherry, where her sister lived.

When Tom reached Cherry he was nearly exhausted. His story touched Fanny's sister, and after seeing to it that he ate a good meal, she bade him rest until the last train left there for Maryland. The boy's clothes by this time were in a wretched condition and as she had boys of about Tom's age, she managed to find some presentable clothing for him to travel further in. He left Cherry on the last train, which reached Washington about noon the following day, where he planned to make his final dash to the North.

Everything went on well for Tom until he reached Washington. He was just about to alight when he espied one of his pursuers standing not many yards away. Whether he was still looking for him, or whether he was traveling on his own accord, Tom did not know. He evidently seemed to be watching for some one when Tom spied him. He had presence of mind to hide himself under a seat and when every one had left the train, he made his exit in another direction.

Tom remained in Washington several days, desiring to make this place his destination, but there was some unknown impulse that urged him on to the metropolis.

While in Washington, he saw many things of

interest. To him, it was a wonderful city. The streets, so beautifully planned, and the innumerable public buildings impressed him greatly.

At midnight a few evenings afterwards, Tom Brinley was well on his way to New York. Arriving there, he was directed by a porter to a good stopping place. He dreaded telling his secret, as he had been warned that as he traveled farther North he would not find his own people as loyal to him as the simple Southern folks were in their sympathetic hearts. So he kept his secret in his breast, and assumed the name of Frank Hope. Frank was his benefactor's Christian name, and Hope was his own fancy,—for he hoped for better things in the future, as he pursued his eventful career.

Tom Brinley soon found work, and also time to devote to his studies. He never permitted an opportunity for mental improvement to slip by. To his notice soon came Hooper's Institute, with its advantages for the pursuance of studies in the evenings after working hours. This suited Tom admirably. And he could be found at his desk at the Institute in the evening, while during the day he worked.

He attracted much attention, both at work and at the Institute. Yet in his great desire to learn he did not consider that he, because of his application to duty, was being admired by those that came in touch with him.

At this time a young colored woman attracted his attention. Tom was now in his seventeenth year. Unassuming and manly, he impressed this modest young colored girl, who, like himself, was taking advantage of an opportunity that the North offered.

One evening as they passed out together, Mary Abbott,—that was her name,—said:

"I have been so interested in this article about this Tom Brinley, whom they are seeking, that I want you to read it."

Tom took the paper calmly and read this headline:

ONE THOUSAND DOLLARS REWARD FOR THE RE-
TURN OF A BLACK BOY WHO IS AN ESCAPED CON-
VICT.

And then the text went on to give his description as to color, height, looks, and so on.

Whether Mary was suspicious or not, Tom did not know. She told him that the paper had been sent to her from the South by friends, who sympathized with the boy, because they knew that he was innocent. They had also told her that in that section if any colored person chanced to attract attention by being ambitious, he would be put out of the way by political renegades.

Much to his dismay, Tom found that he was not even safe in New York. What should he

do? What resort had he? Upon handing the
paper back to Mary, he made no comment upon
it other than that the victim must either be
dangerous or valuable.

Tom found himself occasionally at the side
of this fine-looking young girl. He often saw
a resemblance to his benefactor, Uncle Abbott,
and when she told him of a dear uncle, who was
imprisoned by the same wicked people that
hunted the boy, he longed to tell her his secret,
and how his present opportunity was due to
the big-heartedness of this grand old man.

"Not yet," he thought; "I must first know
how much she cares for me before I do this. I
wish I could tell her of my feeling for her; but
I cannot, without telling my secret; so I must
keep this, too, within my breast."

One day, while delivering packages for the
Bracy firm, for which he worked, Tom came
near running into the arms of Joe Vardam.
He had one package marked, "Mrs. Silas Grant,
East 71st Street." After the maid had taken
the package and he was turning to go, he saw
Joe Vardam enter the house. The politician
did not recognize the lad in uniform, and ever
afterward Tom "kept scarce" (in Joe Vardam's terminology) in that vicinity.

In the meantime Tom and Mary often met
and in time they came to know each other well.
Mary discovered admirable traits in Tom, and

Tom discerned excellent qualities in Mary. Aside from going back to and from school, Tom rarely went out, for he did not know when he might run into Joe Vardam.

Tom was always neatly attired, and presented a pleasing appearance. Wherever he delivered goods for his firm, the people were always satisfied with his service. Some commented upon this, and many an extra dollar he had at the end of the month. He had rented a small room in order to save his money.

To Mary Abbott he spoke but slightly of his past, however great was his yearning to do so. Oftimes he felt that he could trust her with his secret.

Upon Fred Trower's return to the North, he told Grace that he had met a man who informed him that Tom Brinley had been sent to the chain-gang, because he was a thief, an idler, and a dangerous character. But since his description of the man tallied with the appearance of Joe Vardam, Grace would not believe the charges against Tom. She said little to Fred about the matter, however.

Joe Vardam had visited the Grants in the course of his search for Tom. This Grace did not know until after a planned absence, arranged for the purpose of avoiding this man. After she returned, however, she learned that he was in search of Tom Brinley. Then, as if in a vision, she remembered about the woman crying for her lost son,—the black woman of whom the little Grant children had spoken.

Over to the de Forests she went and after speaking to Fanny about the matter, she saw Mandy Brinley and talked with her. After this talk Grace was more than ever convinced of Tom's innocence. For between Fanny and Grace, the conclusion had been established that Joe Vardam was a scheming rascal. So the Grants were kept in ignorance of the whereabouts of Tom's mother. After this visit Grace called frequently to see Fanny, and the friendship between the two grew strong and deep.

CHAPTER XIV

TOM IN LOVE

TIME went on and with it Tom had changed, —having grown taller and stouter. Now he had a certain assurance that he could get by better than at first. He was preparing to graduate from Hooper's Institute in his twentieth year, and because of his brilliancy and oratorical ability, he was given the valedictory, which he felt even now unsafe to accept. So, because he begged to be excused, it passed on to the next.

Meanwhile, he had kept up his friendship with Mary Abbott, and though his tender feeling toward her was manifest, he did not dare to speak to her of his love.

"Mary is so hard to read," he would say to himself. "She always seems so sympathetic in her manner, which somewhat puzzles me. She looks at me so tenderly, when she asks me questions regarding my past, and which I try so hard to evade answering. It has been a great task for me to avoid telling her all in the few years in which I have known her. She has been

99

my only comfort through these long and dreary months.''

Mary Abbott was preparing to be a domestic science teacher. She worked as maid in a private family during the day, and at night attended Hooper's Institute. Having come from the South, where the advantage for such a training was small, her fondest hope was to go back as a teacher, with this added Northern training, which was so much the envy of the ambitious Southern girl. Tom knew that she would be leaving him the following fall and then he would be left absolutely alone. What would he then do without congenial association? How he longed to keep her with him! If he only dared tell her his secret, and have her help him to find some way out of the awful dread that occasionally overwhelmed him!

''After you have gone from me, Mary, and have taken all that is sweet out of my life, if I could only find my dear mother, to whom I might go for solace! I wonder if she still lives and yearns for her boy! O Mother, what cruel fate has severed us,—who have lived so happily together!''

One evening, at a church social, Mary met her aunt, whom she had not seen since she left the South. It was Nanna, the cook who worked for the de Forest family. Once when Mary was visiting her, she told her aunt of the fine young

man whom she had met at the Institute and
how much he reminded her of Mandy the laundress.

"The eyes are so much alike," Mary would
say.

Nanna told her that Mandy was in great distress, as they were seeking the lad who had escaped from the chain-gang and she knew that if
they caught him they would lynch him.

"I do feel so sorry for both," said Mary,
"for I know they both suffer. It is so sad that
those wicked people in the South are not
brought to justice."

"Some day them 'white trash' down there
will get all they are lookin' for bless the
Lord!" returned Nanna.

It was then that Mary began to suspect that
Frank Hope was really Tom Brinley,—Mandy's
son. And she resolved that at the first opportunity, she would reveal her suspicions to Tom.

One day Tom felt that he must give vent to
the pent-up feelings that were getting the better
of him. He felt that he must tell some one. In
his association at the Institute he came in touch
with a number of Catholics. Ofttimes he heard
them speak of confession. Then, too, he remembered that one of the boys had committed
a theft in a thoughtless moment, and when he
thought over what he had done it worried him
so much that he confessed to his priest, whose

influence went far towards making his punishment a slight one. Then, too, he was rid of the dreadful remorse that attends a hidden crime.

Tom thought over all this very seriously, and determined to go to a priest and tell him his sad story.

"I must unbosom my secret self," he would often say to himself, "for I cannot stand this torture much longer."

Mary Abbott noticed that Tom was greatly worried,—that recently he even evaded her presence.

"If I could only help him, I would be so happy. I am almost sure that he is Mandy's boy. I must tell him that I know it and that I want to help him. His mother would mean so much to him. If I could only bring them together without even Nanna knowing it! How I want to help him! Can he not see that I care enough for him not to expose him?" she reasoned.

That Mary might not consider him rude in his great distress Tom dropped her these lines:

DEAR MARY:

   Such a spell of melancholy has come over me, because of a great sorrow in my life, that I would not care to burden you with it. When I feel brighter I shall see you.

                    Yours, etc.,

                         FRANK HOPE.

Two weeks passed, during which time Tom was making up his mind just what course to take to relieve himself of his great burden. He determined that he would see Father Wesser, to whom he had been referred by a Catholic friend. As he was walking toward the parish, he came face to face with Mary Abbott, who, not having completed her course of studies, was on her way to the Institute.

"Why, Mary," remarked Tom, somewhat surprised, "where are you bound for?"

"I am on my way to school," replied the girl.

"And you are out for an evening's walk, I suppose?"

"Not exactly," answered Tom, with a faraway look in his eyes.

"Well, I hope in your melancholia you're not planning to jump into the bay."

"I have had a great sorrow, Mary, which has made me feel quite blue at times; and I was on my way to Father Wesser to confide my troubles in him."

"Confide in me, Frank; I believe that I know your trouble. I have recently surmised it. Do you remember long ago when I handed you that paper that was sent me from the South? Well, from your actions then, from the description, and also from what I have recently heard, I think that you are Tom Brinley."

"O Mary,—don't."

"You will not deny that you are Tom Brinley,—will you?"

"Suppose I do say that I am Tom Brinley; what would you do?"

"What should I do other than sympathize with you,—as I have been doing for the past three years? Now I have a great surprise for you,—one that I wish you to hear of."

Tom looked anxiously into Mary's face.

Mary continued:

"It is your mother that I desire to tell you of. She is laundress in the family with my Aunt Nanna, whom I have only recently found. Now your life I have heard of, as she told Nanna and Nanna in turn told me. You must be very cautious, for the people your mother works for, the de Forests, are great friends of the people whom Joe Vardam stopped with when he was up here searching for you."

Tom's eagerness to see his dear mother knew no bounds. He wanted to go directly to her, no matter what might accrue to him from it, but at the look on Mary's beautiful face when he expressed his rash desire, he yielded to the appeal of her worried countenance and said resignedly:

"All right, Mary. I shall let you arrange a meeting with your own tactfulness. Only let me see my mother as soon as you can."

Mary wondered just how things could be arranged, as Tom's mother seldom went out, and then only when her Aunt Nanna urged her to do so.

Despite Mary's record for punctuality at the Institute, to-night she felt that she could not leave Tom. Nor did he persuade her to leave him,—though he knew that she disliked to miss her classes,—as he felt that he needed her just then so much. So on they walked and talked, hardly noticing where they were going.

CHAPTER XV

TOM BRINLEY RESCUES GRACE ENNERY

WHEN the young people reached Sixty-ninth
Street, they were startled by an alarm of fire.
Mary and Tom quickened their steps and has-
tened to the scene,—in Seventy-first Street.

Volumes of smoke seemed to be pouring forth
from the upper windows of a house. A man
rushed in and a woman met him at the head of
the stairs, pointing above, where they both hastened. Soon he was seen with a child in his
arms. He rested her on the step and went up
again, bringing down this time a young girl.
Neighbors took charge of these. No sooner
had the same man gone up again, than flames
were seen bursting from the windows. The
firemen had not yet arrived, and Tom, forget-
ting for the moment Mary at his side, ran into
the house and up the stairs. He saw that the
man was trying to manage a half-dazed boy
and a young woman, who was partly overcome
by the smoke. Tom, seeing that the man was
tottering under the double load, seized the
woman and brought her down the staircase. As

106

he reached the door a neighbor called to him to bring her into the house where the two girls were being cared for.

As soon as Tom reached the air with the woman, she opened her eyes, and looking into the face of her rescuer, cried,

"Why, Tom,—is this Tom Brinley?"

He recognized the woman as one whom he had seen in his Santa Maria home,—Grace Ennery.

"Yes, ma'am," he replied, "but don't expose me, please."

By this time Fred Trower had reached Grace's side with Jack Grant, whom Grace had insisted upon Fred's rescuing, with the rest of the children, before she permitted him to pay any attention to her.

"Fred," she whispered, "this is the boy whom I sent you in search of. He is the one who prevented us from being overcome by the smoke."

Tom put his finger to his lip in order to quiet her, fearing exposure.

"Give your address to Mr. Trower, and we shall arrange to talk with you, Tom. Do not fear anything, as we shall now,—since you have so bravely rescued us,—guard you with our lives."

"Good-by," whispered Tom, as he handed his address to Mr. Trower and hurried out, not wishing to excite attention. To his amazement, he found that as he pushed his way out of the neighbor's house he was confronted by policemen and reporters. In the street there was much excitement, for by this time the engines had arrived and great crowds had congregated. As Tom appeared upon the street, he was greeted with "Bravo! bravo!" from the crowd. Some came up to him and asked his name; but Tom, being entirely unprepared for this notoriety, brushed quickly by the people, refusing to comment upon what he had done.

"Give ye name, ye fool," cried a tough; "ye might git somethin' out er it."

"Don't want anything," answered Tom.

"Then tell us where you live," interrupted a policeman.

"Don't want to," muttered Tom, and pushing by them, he ran up the street.

"Queer guy!" remarked some one in the crowd.

Tom ran home alone in his excitement, leaving Mary waiting for him somewhere in the crowd.

After the fire had subsided and the Grant children and Grace Ennery were permitted to return home, accompanied by Fred Trower, they were temporarily provided for in the lower part of the house. The fire, caused by the short-circuiting of the electric wires, affected the upper part of the house only, and that part by smoke and water rather than by flames.

When Mr. and Mrs. Grant returned home from a social function, greatly frightened,—as they had been sent for,—the children told them excitedly how a colored man had come to the rescue when Mr. Trower had been almost overcome.

"Who was he, and what was his name?" inquired Mr. and Mrs. Grant, in a breath.

"He wouldn't tell us his name. Did he tell you, Aunt Grace? I saw him talking to you and Mr. Trower," said Jack with much concern.

Grace remained quiet, but Fred Trower broke in:

"He did, but in our excitement we forgot it."

"I thought that I saw him write something down," Margaret put in.

"If he did, I don't really recall it," was Fred's reply.

This conversation was interrupted by the maid, who came in to ask for help in removing some beds to the library. Both Mr. Grant and Fred went out to assist her. After everything had been arranged, Fred left, promising to see Grace on the morrow.

Going directly to the club, Fred remained there talking of the fire and other things until quite a late hour, when he returned home. While undressing for bed, he thought of the exciting events of the evening and of the bravery of Tom Brinley.

"Brave chap!" said Fred aloud, as was his custom in the quiet of his apartment. "I wonder if such a fellow could be a dangerous character. Nevertheless, I'll size him up to-morrow, and will let Grace know what I think of him. Let me see where he lives."

Fred arose, took up his vest and to his great dismay found that the paper was not where he was sure he had placed it. He looked in the other pockets of the clothes that he wore; still he could not find it. His first impulse, of course, was to call up Grace and ask her if she had found the slip of paper that Tom Brinley had given her.

Immediately he went to the 'phone and called up the Grant house. Of course, at this hour of the night, Mr. Grant was the one to answer the call, as all the servants were asleep in another part of the house. A night call always annoyed Silas Grant, as he never cared to be aroused from his sleep. And when both he and his wife were wakened by the ring just outside their door, he remarked:

"Who the devil is calling up at this hour of the night,—after all the excitement, too?"

"I can't imagine," replied his wife. "Probably some one who has just heard of the fire and is calling up to see if we are all right. Get up, Silas, and see who it is.''

Mr. Grant arose reluctantly, and after inquiring who it was and finding out that it was Fred Trower, said:

"What in the thunder do you want to wake us up at this hour of the night for?"

"Awful sorry to bother you, Grant, but I must speak to Miss Ennery upon a matter of very great importance."

"Very great importance, hey? And can't wait until a decent hour to talk to her," snarled Silas Grant. And as he walked through the hall to Miss Ennery's door he muttered: "Wakin' up everybody for a little nonsense."

Grace awoke when Mr. Grant called to her, and impatiently slipping on her boudoir slippers and gown, went to the 'phone.

"Fred, why could you not wait? Mr. Grant does not like this intrusion on his sleep."

"Sorry, Grace, but I could not wait until morning to tell you that I lost the paper with Tom's address on it. Did you find it after I left you?"

"O Fred, how careless of you! What will you do? Something must be done immediately."

"What can I do? I don't know where to find him. I didn't notice what was on the card."

"O Fred, this is dreadful! I'll look around and call you up if I find it. If you don't hear from me, come up to the house before you go to your office and we can determine upon some step to take under these unfortunate circumstances. Good-by for the present."

Grace, depressed, went on a search for the paper which would, however, mean much if found before it fell into another's hand. Joe Vardam had made the name of Tom Brinley well known in the Grant home, as he had stayed with them when he was searching for Tom. As has been said when Grace heard of his coming, she purposely,—without letting the Grants into the secret,—made a visit to a school chum, to avoid identification.

And now the only thing to do was to find the card for should any of the Grants get hold of the paper, it would surely mean a return to the chain-gang for the boy.

Poor Grace searched everywhere for the missing slip of paper, but it failed to materialize. She refrained from inquiring whether or not it had been seen, as she knew that she would surely incur suspicion. Tired and fagged out from the hunt, she returned to her room a most unhappy woman.

Fred called early the next day and they talked seriously of some possible way to save the boy. They could arrive at nothing definite, and Fred left as quietly as he had entered, promising to think things over and return in the evening.

CHAPTER XVI

SPIRITED AWAY

IN the morning's papers much space was devoted to the fire in the Grant household, and there was also a statement to this effect:

A colored youth, whose name could not be ascertained, saved Miss Ennery, the artist (whom reports state will soon marry Banker Trower's son). Fred Trower and Jack Grant were also saved from being overcome. Fred Trower knew at his last going up into the burning apartment that he would have to bring both Miss Ennery and little Jack down, for he was afraid that to leave either would mean sure death to that one. When the colored youth rushed up, he found that Trower's load was too much for him, so, relieving him of Miss Ennery, he enabled Trower to rescue the boy, which was all that he could well do in his overcome condition. Detectives are hunting for the youth, whom the Grants feel should be rewarded.

Grace came down to her breakfast with a careworn look. Mrs. Grant insisted that the girl remain in bed and a physician be summoned; but Grace said she was not ill.

"What is the matter with you then?" inquired Mrs. Grant. "You look positively wretched. You must have attention."

"I thank you, Mrs. Grant, but I must be out to-day; it is important that I should go."

114

"O Grace, you must not go out; you have had a dreadful shock, and it is telling upon you. Let me do your errand."

"It is so dear of you, Mrs. Grant, but I shall go to bed when I return."

"O Dad," cried Jack, running into the dining-room, all excited, his face very red, "I have found the escaped criminal in my bed!"

Every one was startled and stopped eating to look at Jack. But before any one had a chance to question him, he read aloud:

Tom Brinley, No. 88 —— Street.

The shock was great for Grace, for she had not looked for the exposure in this way. Nevertheless she had presence of mind not to say anything as Jack handed the slip of paper to his father.

"How the devil did this get here?" he asked in a perplexed manner.

"Oh," cried Margaret "that looks like the slip of paper the colored man handed to Mr. Trower,—doesn't it, Aunt Grace?"

"Does it? I was so full of excitement that I did not take notice of what he gave Mr. Trower."

Then excusing herself, Grace hurried to her room, put on her coat and hat, and went out immediately. At the nearest telephone station she called up Fred Trower, arranging for him to meet her immediately. This Fred did in a remarkably short time, and away they went to find the address that Grace bore in mind, for Jack had read it in a very audible manner.

They found the place, but the youth was not at home. Gaining the desired information as to his place of employment, and finding out his assumed name, they called for him at the Bracy establishment.

When Tom heard the news that he was wanted he thought that his hour had come, and as he went into the presence of Fred and Grace, he prepared himself for the inevitable.

They took Tom aside and told him what had happened.

"You must leave immediately, as you are in danger, for these Grants are friends of Vardam's," remarked Grace excitedly.

As if he had been struck with a bolt, Tom recalled the fact that he had delivered a package at this very house, and had come almost face to face with the man who had done him so much wrong.

Grace looked up into her lover's face, saying:

"Suppose, Fred, we send him out of the country? What boats are going out this morning?"

"Let me see—the *Lusanne* sails at twelve o'clock to-day. Do you think he can make it?"

"Why not?" interposed Grace. "Tom, ask the manager to let you off at our request and we shall see that you get there in time."

Tom obediently did as he was bid, yet in his heart at that moment he was prepared to face the worst.

He was relieved from duty without any trouble, and, giving him money to get suitable clothing for the trip, Grace and Fred left him to meet him again at the *Lusanne's* dock.

As they had a little time, Grace bought for the boy a number of things that she felt he would enjoy having and yet knew he would not get. She had warned him not to return to his stopping place, since she did not know what course Mr. Grant would take.

Grace and Fred were anxiously waiting at the dock when Tom reached there, and having him register as Lester Trower, the name of Fred's dead brother, they supplied him with funds to give him a start at Oxford, where Grace wished him to continue his studies.

Remaining until they saw the boat fairly under way, and with the feeling of security that came of seeing the deep lying between Tom and his enemies, Grace and Fred left the wharf, a happy pair.

"Now, Grace," said Fred, "let us arrange for a quiet wedding in a few days, since your father has given his consent and tells us not

to wait for him, as his stay is still indefinite.
For a time we can rent an apartment; it's easy
enough to make a change when we have found a
suitable location. I have a notion that Vardam
will be up here in a few days, and I want you
to be out of his way. To-day is Wednesday.
Let us be married Saturday in the Little
Church Around the Corner.''

"All right, Fred; perhaps it is the proper
thing now. And the coming true of my wish
has made me so happy. Yet we never have
what we really want, after all, in this life.
Things happen so differently from what we
desire. I wanted to talk with Tom about his
trouble. I firmly believe he met with foul play.
Some one wished to do him harm.''

"Yes, Grace, I, too, believe in the lad now,
since I have seen him and know of his unselfish-
ness. He seems utterly incapable of wrong-do-
ing. His eyes are so wonderfully sympathetic.
Poor boy! If he is truly innocent,—as I believe
him to be,—his persecutors should be brought
to justice.''

"Fred, you had better leave me now and return to the office while I go home and rest.''

"You need rest surely, for you look so careworn. Go home, and do not worry any more,
but get yourself together for the event of our
lives,—our wedding.''

Grace smiled complacently as they parted,

Fred going to the office, and she home to rest,— both pleased with the fact that they were able to beat whomever would be first on the boy's trail.

At the dinner-table Grace learned that detectives had already been on the boy's track and that a telegram had been sent to Vardam to acquaint him of the fact.

"I can't see for the life of me," remarked Mr. Grant at the dinner-table, "how that paper could have gotten into my house, unless it was brought in. I shan't rest until I find out the truth."

In the meantime Fred had arranged for a Saturday morning wedding. A dear little apartment, overlooking the Park was the selected spot,—for a while at least.

Fred's father and mother were pleased with the match, for they both knew and respected Banker Ennery's daughter. They had met Grace and liked her, and were very proud of the fact that Fred was attracted toward such a fine girl.

After dinner Grace found Mrs. Grant in her apartment, and told her that she and Fred had decided to be married very quietly the following Saturday, and that she wanted to have her and Mr. Grant present with the children. She also said that Fanny de Forest would be at the ceremony.

"I am glad you are going to marry, Grace," she replied, "but I hope you won't go to work and settle down and never amount to anything socially. Why, even your father went out more frequently than you do."

"That will depend entirely upon Fred, Mrs. Grant. If he cares for society, of course I will adapt myself to his inclinations along this line."

"Oh, he used to go out a good bit, Grace; but since he has been so wrapped up in you, he has not been seen anywhere but at the club."

"Well, I suppose that this and other things will adjust themselves. Nevertheless, what we do socially, and otherwise, I hope will be for the best."

"Saturday morning then, Grace, my dear," remarked Mrs. Grant as Grace arose to go.

When Grace rang the de Forest bell that very afternoon she was pleased to have the door opened by Mandy Brinley. In handing her card to Mandy, Grace said softly:

"Come to this place alone to-night—I must see you regarding Tom."

Mandy bowed understandingly, and hastened to call Miss de Forest, who soon put in her appearance, bedecked like the Queen of Sheba.

"Ah," she cried in her usual spirited manner, "what wind blew you my way to-day, you naughty kid?"

"I'm marrying on Saturday morning, Fanny, in the Little Church Around the Corner, and I want you present as a witness."

"Sure thing, kid, and I wish you piles of luck. You're getting the real stuff, Grace. Lots of girls have been crazy over him,—got the dough, you know (that is, his dad has, and he the only child). He's some catch, I tell you! Why didn't you have a decent wedding? What's it so quick for? Did the fire drive you to it?"

"No, not exactly," drawled Grace, "and in a way it did. Then, since we were really going to cross the Rubicon, and neither of us cared about a large wedding, we thought we might as well cross now as at any time."

"Well, perhaps you're right. After all, Grace, what's in a wedding? It's the living afterwards that counts in the long run. By the way, they've found Mandy's poor son, haven't they?"

Grace, reddening a bit, replied:

"Yes."

"Mrs. Grant said that they found his card after the fire, and some think he was the lad who rescued you."

"That may be so," said Grace.

"If you could hear his poor mother talk, you would think he was an angel instead of the devil Vardam pictures him to be. Well, I don't know; it's all very mysterious,—that he should be so good and at the same time so bad.''

Grace went after Fanny had lavished all sorts of good wishes upon her.

Fanny de Forest was a typical society girl, yet she had a sympathy which Grace thought appealing, and even though Fanny loved to go into society, at every chance she sought Grace and took great delight in her company and in her art. She had a freedom of speech that was attractive in her, though at times she gave it rein until it trampled over the proprieties. Despite this she never, because of her intuitive sympathy, gave offense. Her wholesomeness, combined with this sympathy, had won Grace's friendship.

CHAPTER XVII

THE WEDDING

SATURDAY morning arrived, and upon this eventful day the Grant household was in great excitement. The children did not feel very happy over losing their Aunt Grace, yet they enjoyed the privilege of attending a wedding.

"Aunt Grace, why can't Mr. Trower come here to live? We'll have room for him after the carpenters get through mending where the fire burned," lisped little Elleen, of whom the household always stood in fear; for no one knew just how frankly she would express her views.

"I shall ask him, Elleen," Grace answered, trying hard to keep back a smile which was forcing its way to the front, while little Elleen, ignorant of the amusement she was causing, continued: "If he doesn't want to go upstairs with Sally and Ann, he can have my bed and I will come in with you."

"You are very, very generous, my dear, and your arrangements will be looked into," Grace replied, while taking her into her arms and fondling her closely.

123

The day was a wonderfully pretty one in April. The sun shone as perfectly and the air was as balmy as a day in June, and every one seemed in good spirits. Grace was attired in a simple but handsome traveling suit of pearl gray. Business was very pressing and Fred's father did not wish him to leave for any lengthy absence just then, so the bridal pair had planned a short honeymoon trip to Atlantic City.

Mr. Grant returned to the house at eleven-thirty with his chauffeur and all were ready to be taken over to the church.

When the party had reached the church and were about to alight, they noticed some sort of excitement, which seemed unaccountable.

As soon as they had alighted and entered upon the scene, Mr. Grant found that the detectives whom he had engaged to hunt Tom Brinley, had traced Fred Trower as an accomplice to his flight and a warrant had been issued for his arrest.

Everything was in confusion. Fred's father was distracted; Mr. Grant nonplussed.

The detectives then told how Fred and a lady answering the description of Miss Ennery had gone to Tom Brinley's place of abode the morning that the card was found in the Grant home. The detectives had also found out that the boy had been posing under the name of Frank

Hope, and that he had been in the community several years. He had worked for the Bracy firm, and since he had been North had entered and graduated from Hooper's Institute. They also discovered that, the morning he disappeared, a man and woman, answering to the description of Fred Trower and Miss Ennery had been with him. The three had been traced to the wharf of the *Lusanne,* upon which boat, they learned, the boy had taken passage under the name of Lester Trower.

Grace Ennery and Fred Trower stood speechless during this rehearsal. Both failed to show any emotion, while Mrs. Trower sobbed and Mrs. Grant, between outbursts, stated how terrible it was to bring upon them such disgrace because of a worthless "Nigger."

"Why don't you talk, Fred?" inquired his father.

"I will, Dad, when the time comes. Come on in and let the ceremony go on."

A sadder group never entered a church for a wedding. Mr. Grant remained with the detectives, while the others went forward, where the few witnesses sat.

After the ceremony the Grant children and Mrs. Grant left immediately for their home, while Mr. Grant, the two detectives, Grace, her husband, and Mr. and Mrs. Trower were driven over to the station, where Fred's father ar-

ranged matters so that he and his bride could
have an unmolested honeymoon.

Fanny de Forest dismissed her own chaf-
feur, at Mrs. Grant's request, and rode in the
car with her and the children, so that they might
have an opportunity to talk over the event that
had just transpired.

"Well, even if Fred and Grace did spirit the
boy away, I don't believe that he was the devil
old Vardam said he was," Fanny replied, after
a short silence, having learned the facts of the
case.   Then she went on: "Did they admit
doing what they were charged with?"

"No, not one word did either of them utter
regarding the affair," returned Mrs. Grant.
"Fred Trower said that he would talk when
the time came. I don't understand it one bit,
Fanny."

"Do you think, since they cannot get the boy,
that they will ever take Fred into custody?"
asked Fanny, with a serious look.

"Never! Jail Fred Trower for a Nigger?
The only inconvenience he would experience
would be a long-drawn-out trial perhaps, as it
would be interstate. And about all they could
do would be to fine Fred for interference with
the law."

"Poor Fred,—I believe he is doing it all for
her! She is so unprejudiced in her feelings, so
loyal! She has a strong flow of anti-slavery

blood running through her. Her mother's ancestors, I have been told, came over in the *Mayflower*," remarked Fanny seriously; to which Mrs. Grant hastily replied:

"Yes, but her father and his people were Southern slaveholders. Well, at any rate, it is very mysterious, how they knew him, and how the fatal card was brought into my house."

By this time Fanny's home was reached, and she alighted, promising to see Mrs. Grant and the children soon.

The children, not having understood all that had transpired, sat as quiet as mice all the way, until Fanny alighted, when little Elleen called to her:

"Does the colored woman still cry for her boy who was stolen from her, Aunt Fanny?"

This Fanny pretended not to hear, as she had never mentioned to Mrs. Grant that her laundress was the mother of Tom Brinley. Mandy Brinley, as Fanny knew, was so afraid of Vardam that she wanted him never to know what became of her. Thus she defended Mandy's whereabouts not only from Vardam but also from his friends, the Grants.

When Fanny reached home she was very happy to find Mandy and tell her that her son had escaped to England. She could not account for the fact that Mandy was not as overjoyed as she expected she would be.

"Ain't you glad, Mandy?" asked Fanny.

" 'Deed I is, 'deed I is," replied the poor woman, trying to assume an air of surprise; but the truth was that she met Grace by appointment the very night Grace called at Fanny's home, and had exchanged confidences both regarding the boy and the crookedness of the politics of Santa Maria, which would take advantage of a lad so ambitious as was Tom.

CHAPTER XVIII

THE TRIAL

In spite of the cloud that hung over the heads of Grace and Fred, they spent a delightful honeymoon by the sea. Tom's name was rarely mentioned, for new scenes and new conditions had brought about new thoughts.

While they were away Fred's mother superintended the arrangement of their apartment. Grace's furniture and effects, which were brought from her rooms at the Grants' home, were artistically arranged. The evening they were expected home being chilly and stormy, Mrs. Trower had a cheerful fire made in the grate, and both she and her husband eagerly awaited the arrival of their children.

Supper was waiting when the honeymooners arrived, and they, with the older folks, enjoyed it immensely. Every sad thought seemed far away until Fred's father aroused him to serious thought by asking him how he came to entangle himself with the colored runaway.

Then he and Grace together told the story of Tom Brinley.

129

"This Joe Vardam is expected on to the trial, which takes place next week," Fred's father informed them.

"Father, I could bring back this lad and turn him over into the hands of these scoundrels, but I won't. Why, his landlady, Hooper's Institute, and the Bracy firm belie every statement to the effect that he is a dangerous character."

The trial was set for the Monday morning after Grace and Fred returned home, but, owing to the fact that Vardam could not be present, it was postponed.

"He can't find any witnesses, I suppose," Fred remarked to Grace the next evening, as they sat at dinner in their apartment.

During the interim Fred gathered all his witnesses, who included all whom the lad had come in touch with since his escape to the North.

Fred was impressed with the fact that they were all eager to appear in behalf of his protégé.

At length Vardam and his witnesses came North, and the day of the trial was set for 10 o'clock of the morning after their arrival.

Mr. Grant, with Vardam, Tilton and their lawyer, were in court and seated long before the appointed time.

Fred, with Grace and their lawyer, made

their appearance. Their witnesses included all with whom Tom had been associated since his coming North, also his mother. The courtroom was packed with society folk as well as with those who did not mingle with the upper strata. The unique feature of this case was that wealthy society leaders were defending a Negro runaway at a time when prejudice was so violent.

The judge took his place on the bench and called for order in the court.

He read in measured tones the charge against Fred Trower, who was accused of the abduction of a criminal for whom extradition papers had been made out, and of placing him, under an assumed name, out of the reach of the law.

Then Fred was asked to take the stand. He did so, testifying as to the Grant fire and his meeting Tom there for the first time. He gave a graphic account of the boy's rescue of Miss Ennery and Jack Grant at a time when he, Fred, was almost exhausted, and he told how the coming of this black lad on the scene had prevented all three from being overcome by the smoke.

This news was a shock to Mr. Grant, as he did not for a moment think that Tom Brinley was the rescuer of whom he had heard so much, yet he recovered his poise.

After Fred had finished, Grace was called to the stand. She told of her meeting the lad for the first time in Santa Maria,—an innocent boy, with a desire to be something in the world. She told of the child's love for his Leader, who had died, and of the great prejudice she saw existing between the races. She even went so far as to tell of her conversation with the pursuer of the lad and of what Tom had told her of Vardam. The lawyer on the other side tried to rule out this testimony, but her lawyer showed that it was in order.

Then Tom's landlady was called, and she spoke of the lad's fine qualities and business integrity. The Bracy firm in turn told of the excellent service Tom had given them and how much they appreciated it.

The last witness in Tom's behalf was his mother. She spoke in somewhat broken Southern style, but with earnestness so sincere that it impressed all present to such a degree that one could hear a pin drop during her testimony.

Mandy told of Tom's visit to the Leader's grave, which was constantly kept fresh with flowers. She said that he went over and found the flowers withered the day she last saw him. As he was going he said, "Ma, I'm goin' over to git flowers for de Leader's grave out of the fields of San Joan." She stated that after that she saw him no more.

Tilton and Vardam were very restless in their seats, as they listened to the words that their opponents were uttering in behalf of a member of a race that they hated with all their hearts.

Vardam was then called upon, and he arose to his feet. Clearing his throat, he told of every conceivable guilt he could name that the Blacks were associated with. He spoke of black men's assaulting white women, of the Negro's neglect, idleness, and laziness, of their feigning good behavior when the Northern whites were around and of the latter's interference with the Southern laws, making the Negro contemptuous, and hard to manage by his Southern employers.

"May I ask," interrupted the judge, "what this Tom Brinley was sent to the chain-gang for?"

Vardam cleared his throat and replied:

"He was surly, rude, idle, and a dangerous character."

"Did I not hear that he stole?"

"Oh, yes," Vardam quickly responded.

"What did he steal?"

"A number of things."

"Name some of them."

"I object," interposed Vardam's lawyer.

"If I can have one concrete example to place him in the criminal class, I can see where Frederick Trower and his wife protected a criminal. But up to this point, I cannot see where he has been a dangerous character in the community."

"Well, I tell you they are all dangerous,—
every confounded one of them."

"That is sufficient," said the judge.

Then Tilton was called to the witness chair.

"What do you know of Tom Brinley," asked
the judge.

"Everything bad," answered Tilton, rather
glumly.

"What connection did he have with you?"

"He worked for me."

At this remark Mandy Brinley sobbed aloud,
for she knew that Tom had never laid eyes upon
this man that stood there, lying.

"What work did he do?"

"Worked in my rice-fields, and while there
he created disturbances among the other workers."

"Then," remarked the judge, "do I understand that you sent him, for no particular offense, to the chain-gang, where after being
driven and lashed and starved, he loosens his
chains, steals tools from the drunken guard,
beats him into unconsciousness, and escapes?
That is what any of us would have done under
the circumstances."

At this moment the court-room door opened
and Tom Brinley walked slowly down the aisle.
Those who knew him could not have been more
startled. Tom's mother screamed out, and Joe

Vardam turned as white as a ghost, as Tom stood there facing the judge.

"Your honor," said he, "I, Tom Brinley, have come back to defend myself."

Vardam, regaining command of himself, caught Tom by the arm and cried:

"You are my prisoner!"

"Order in the court-room," cried the judge. "Release that boy. He is yours only if he is proven guilty." Then, turning to the boy, he asked: "What have you to say, boy?"

The unexpected arrival of the youth,—regarding whom so many conflicting reports had been heard,—was dramatic. He descended upon the court like a bolt from the blue. Every eye was riveted upon him; his face and bearing were closely scrutinized; his manner of speaking, his every gesture was eagerly watched.

And what did the audience in the court-room see? A manly youth of twenty, whose very appearance belied the accusations of Vardam and Tilton. They saw a brown-colored boy, with a broad brow that was crowned with curly black hair; with large, glowing, brown eyes that could flash with indignation or melt with tenderness; with a nose slightly Roman in character; a jaw and chin broad and square; lips firmly compressed, and a face round and full. But the determination that was expressed in that firm mouth and square jaw and chin were

relieved from harshness by the twinkle in his
eye. And those slightly curved lips could
break into a beautiful smile. Not exactly a
handsome face, yet it was a decidedly noble
one. Suffering and sorrow showed there; but
it was suffering and sorrow that had been con-
quered and mastered that was expressed in that
countenance.

And the form they saw was in keeping with
the head and face; a form slightly above the
medium height, erect, broad-shouldered and
deep-chested, with that ease of movement that
betokens great strength and agility.

It was easily seen that Tom had made a
favorable impression upon his audience before
he began to speak in calm, measured tones, with
a well-modulated voice.

Amid breathless silence Tom began his story.

He told a most touching tale of his life with
his mother at Santa Maria, stating that he
did all that he could to help her. He told the
court how Vardam laid in wait for him, as was
his habit with other ambitious individuals of
his race. He told a pitiful tale of the chain-
gang, having sufficient presence of mind not to
mention Uncle Abbott; yet he did say that he
found others there as innocent of crime as he
was. He said, in reference to the overseer
whom he incapacitated, that he had hoped in
his escape to meet no obstacle and that when

he did meet such in the form of the overseer, that to deal this blow was his only salvation, his only gateway to liberty.

In finishing his story, Tom said that he had an opportunity in his trip to Europe to escape, but when the disabled *Lusanne* stopped off Nova Scotia for repairs,—she having been hurt by storm,—on going ashore he had learned from a New York paper that his benefactors were in trouble because of him. Then he felt that he must return to exonerate these good friends from any blame.

The verdict was written on the faces of the jury as they filed out. While awaiting their return, Tom sat facing the court. He was not conscious of the opinions the people were forming of him; but sat there stoically calm and self-possessed.

CHAPTER XIX

TOM BRINLEY AT OXFORD

EVERY one in the court-room could not escape some feeling of relief when, after a great suspense, the jury returned with a verdict of "Not Guilty."

For a second everything was silent, and then excitement reigned. It seemed that every one sympathized with Grace and her husband and the lad who had so nobly defended himself.

Tom's mother could not release the boy from her embrace, for her joy at seeing him and knowing that he had his liberty was almost too much for her. All she could utter in her great emotion was:

"My Tom,—Ma's own Tom!"

Vardam and Tilton were absolutely without sympathizers. For every word from Tom's mouth had touched the hearts in the court, as he defended his actions with so much depth of feeling. And even though he was a colored boy trying to prove his innocence, one was moved as he gazed into his deep-set eyes, for in their depths his very soul revealed itself.

138

All said something encouraging to him, and in his simple, unassuming way, he passed out by the side of his mother.

Once outside, Grace urged Tom to go on his trip as soon as his mother felt that she could spare him. This he promised to do. Freed now, he was able to do those things that had been impossible to him before, because of his fear of detection.

What enjoyment Tom took in being able to look the world squarely in the face! The feeling of independence that possessed him could not be expressed in words.

Mr. Silas Grant forsook his Southern friends, for one could see that, apart from the conventional courtesies that he was bound to extend to them, he was eager to be freed of their society.

Silas Grant made it his business to see Tom in a few days and offer to share a portion of his educational expenses. And even after Tom told him that Mr. and Mrs. Trower had amply provided for him, he still proffered his services. Upon his insistence, Tom asked him if he would devote that portion to the comfort of his mother. Mr. Grant said that he was willing to do so, because he felt he must do something for a lad,—even though he was black,—who had been so brave in rescuing one of his children at the time of the fire.

Tom found some time to spend with the companion of his dark days, Mary Abbott. He told her much,—considering the short time he had,—of his feeling for her, and of his desire to make her his wife when he made good. He also told her of her Uncle Abbott, his benefactor, and how he wished that it were in his power to do something for him.

Having attended to all the necessary things,—among them the adopting of his right name in every instance where the name of Frank Hope had been used,—in two weeks' time, in company with his mother and Mary Abbott, Tom stood on the same wharf, again starting after bidding them fond good-bys to carve a destiny for himself in another land.

The steamer *Excelsior,* after an uneventful trip, landed in Liverpool about a week after Tom had embarked. When he reached London he could hardly discern his hand before his face.

"This is one of those dense fogs of which London is famous," he said. "Your welcome is not an enthusiastic one, but, old London, I have faith in you, and in your people, and in your laws."

London was a wonderful city to Tom,—so different from the great metropolis that he had just left. The streets so narrow, the crowds so dense, and everywhere people,—great hordes of people.

"The war's killing off of millions does not seem to have produced a scarcity here, at least," remarked Tom to himself.

Everywhere England, the motherland, was in gala attire, because of her great victory. Even though the war had been over some little time, the gay-colored buntings gave evidence of the recent triumphant end of the fight.

This condition of things surprised Tom, for he expected to see nearly every one in mourning, because of the great numbers he had read of who had been slain in battle,—who surely, thought Tom, must have had association with every other person alive.

Tom, in his inexperience, did not realize that this is but the condition that succeeds any great calamity. So quickly are the horrors forgotten that one often wonders with alarm at the indifference to the taking of human life.

Tom was greatly impressed with the treatment he received in this great city. Deference and respect lined his pathway. Nowhere was he made to feel that he was different from any one else. As he wrote to Mary Abbott:

I feel so different here. There is no prejudice anywhere. My color appears to be only an accident, as does the color of one's hair or eyes. I may exaggerate conditions, Mary, but it seems as if the English people are extremely courteous because I am

colored,—their desire seeming to be to make me disregard the
fact that I am different from other people. I feel that I should
like to remain here and never come back to my country, where
I am spurned and treated as though I were responsible for that
for which God alone is accountable.

Tom established himself with a very pleasant
English family, all the members of which were
extremely kind to him; and after a few days he
gained admittance to the great English University, Oxford.

He was delighted with this old English institution, from which had sprung some of the
greatest scholars the world has ever known.
Every instructor was keen, earnest, and sincere.
Every student had an equal chance. The great
war affected this institution very little, for within its walls all races and nations were represented. As time went on, Tom met many interesting characters,—among them, some Afri-
cans, who were enrolled there. There was one
Siami,—a brilliant Negro, black as the Ace of
Spades, but as rich as Crœsus; his father was
king of a tribe in his native land, and the vast
territory upon which he lived was rich in gold
mines. Of him Tom wrote home:

He mingles with royalty and has advantages over the white
man without a title, for he is admitted into inner royal circles,
and upon festive occasions he takes precedence of those who
are below a king in rank.

Tom's letters were always interesting, and
Mrs. Trower, Mary Abbott, and his mother

were his constant correspondents. As for Grace Trower, she was enthusiastic over Tom's letters, and the zeal with which the boy took up his work.

Westminster Abbey, wherein are buried all the English celebrities, was the place in which Tom loved to wander. For hours he would sit and study this last resting-place of England's famed sons, awed and impressed by its silent grandeur.

Mary Abbott kept Tom in touch with his country's activities. After he was away two years, great excitement was being manifested over the country's threatened war with Japan. Then, too, the question that his people were pressing was "The admittance of the Negro into the State Militia." "No," cried many; "Yes," cried a few. "What are we," exclaimed Tom, on reading of the issue, "that even to die for one's country is too great an honor?"

Tom, on account of his excellent record, was admitted into some of the most exclusive societies of the University. He was even privileged to attend social functions. The social attitude of the English people puzzled him, for he thought that socially his color would be a barrier as long as he lived, so far as mingling with white man was concerned. Though enjoying every privilege, Tom never took ad-

vantage of this liberty given him, and he seldom
entered into the social life that he was so often
urged to share.

Mrs. Trower did not stint Tom at all in the
matter of allowance. She was eager for him
to imbibe all he could from educational sources.
She encouraged him to visit historic places
throughout Europe. Although the war had
left its mark of devastation to a greater or
less degree on the different countries, she felt,
nevertheless, that he could picture in his
imagination what it had been.

It was interesting to Tom to watch the
women in the different avenues of work, which
before had been filled by men. Outside of England women predominated. Everywhere he
went Tom was forced to the conclusion that she
could never be denied the ballot for which she
had fought so arduously. He found, however,
upon investigation, that in nearly every country that had participated in the war the women
had been permitted to vote. Only England was
still orthodox in this particular, and her Pank-
hursts were still knocking at the door of Parlia-
ment and the House of Commons, but without
success, even though much progress had been
made by the feminists.

"Why is it," asked Tom of an English friend,
"that the women are so persistent and rash

in their demands?" For they still made raids upon assembled political bodies.

Felton, the Englishman to whom he had put the question, answered:

"We English do not comply with the requests of our women, without forethought. We do not believe that it is good for women to have what we have decided is not good for them. Our attitude towards our women is the same as the Southern attitude is towards your people. We believe that women should always be subservient to men, and to place the ballot in their hands would surely make them the equal of men; and that we Englishmen do not wish."

Whereupon Tom inquired:

"How is it that the countries all about have granted her this privilege?"

"So many would not have done so, if it had not been for the war, which, taking so many of their men, necessarily made the countries, to a great degree, dependent upon their women," was the reply.

Tom had many leisure hours while in England, and in them he often thought of his dear ones so far from him, and of his beloved Leader's grave. His greatest sorrow was the fact that he never could feel safe to return to his own home town and visit this spot, which he knew had been long neglected.

"How long," he would ask in his sorrowful

mood, "will Vardam and Tilton hold their cruel sway because of politics?"

Not many days after one of his periods of thinking of Santa Maria he received a letter from Mary, who was then teaching in a Southern school. In it she sent a newspaper clipping, which read as follows:

The Vance Institute has closed its doors. So indifferent were its students to what the great John Vance saw fit to leave for an unworthy people that it could not continue to open its doors to emptiness.

In the letter Mary stated that politics had grown so rotten in and around Santa Maria that the appropriation left in trust had been misused, and that there were no funds left to keep this greatest of Southern Institutes open to the people that it was intended to help. Then she added:

If some one could have followed the Leader, who, like him, had the love of his people at heart, things would not have taken the course that they did.

"Following the Leader," breathed Tom. "Could I but do this, Mary, it would be the realization of my dearest wish. But I cannot follow the Leader in Santa Maria. If I follow him, it must be elsewhere."

Time passed and Tom made many good friends. He applied himself arduously to his studies, never feeling that he could spend any time for those things that did not tend to advance him along the road toward the responsibility that Mrs. Trower had made his goal.

Mary still continued to keep Tom in touch with American affairs. Her letters were a great source of delight to the student, because they were so full of cheer and encouragement. And there were times in Tom's life as well as in the life of other ambitious individuals, when the worker needed a cheering word from home, for they served as stimulants along life's rugged paths.

Tom's mother was still with the de Forests, who were extremely good to her. Often she wrote to Tom that the Grant children kept her cheerful, and that Mrs. Grant constantly looked after her wants. Grace Trower always inquired after Mandy when she went to see Fanny, who had become her very dear friend.

"Grace kid," Fanny would say, in her usual buoyant manner, "you are the real dope. I want you always to be where I can get to you easy, if I'm in bad. You'll always fix me up. You know what you're up to every time, kid, and that's more than a lot o' them know."

Four years had passed since Tom set sail for England, and time had wrought many changes. Margaret Grant was a young woman, out of school, and ready to be launched into the world of fashion by a society-loving mamma, and to

be kept upon this social sea by a rich papa.
Jack, whom Tom Brinley helped Fred Trower
to rescue from the fire, was off to Yale, shining,
as most Jacks do, in the athletic field. Elleen
did not sing "Eeny, Meeny, Miney Mo" now,
but had stolen over to Fanny's and hunted
Mandy, to whom she had become much attached.
And the greatest of all changes was that Silas
Grant had become a director of the Negro Protective Federation.

And in the Trower household noteworthy
changes had taken place too. Here you will find
a baby girl of three prattling around in mer-
riest glee. She has made the Trower happiness
complete, and Grandpa Ennery gets a generous
portion of happiness under the spell of Baby
Edythe's winsome smiles. And this little one
knows Tom Brinley, because of her mother's
talks of him, especially at this time, when in
her home much is being said concerning the ad-
visibility of Tom's return.

CHAPTER XX

THE Trowers showed great interest in Tom Brinley's letters. The unprejudiced condition abroad appealed to them particularly, and for that reason they were convinced that Tom, having completed his Oxford course, could not do more wisely than cast his lot under England's skies.

As for Tom, he was eager to return, but he could not decide what to do.

"The North does not need me; her colleges and universities are open to the Negro, but positions are closed to him; therefore, there is nothing for me to do there," he thought.

The Negro Protective Federation had its quota of Negro men employed, he learned on inquiry, yet the many advantages offered Tom in England compensated in a measure for his disappointment. They did not wholly satisfy him, however. He wanted to see his mother and Mary, whom he had not grown to care for one whit less.

Grace Trower was eager to see what Oxford

149

had done for Tom, and hoped that he might venture to return and engage in active life in the South; but she became thoroughly convinced that such a move would be foolish on his part, when a paper from Santa Maria was sent to Mr. Grant, and he in turn sent it over to her. This paper stated that if Tom Brinley, the Negro ex-convict, ever planted foot upon land below the Mason and Dixon line,—while the present political party was in power,—he would again be immediately seized and put into the chain-gang, where he and his whole race belonged.

"That is dreadful!" cried Grace, after she had read the extract to her husband.

"Dweadful! dweadful!" lisped little Edythe, who, apparently, took it all in.

"We had better send him this paper and advise him to remain on the other side until things look more favorable over here. He, no doubt, will very easily find something to do."

Tom, on receipt of the information, decided that his lot must be cast in Europe.

"When I get money enough I shall send for Mary and marry her; and we will spend the rest of our lives over here," he mused.

Having developed into a powerfully built man by this time, Tom was devoted to athletics, and because of his prowess had gained much honor at Oxford.

On the completion of his course at the University a position was offered him in the newspaper world. *The London Times,*—being a daily paper of large circulation, paying its employees well,—gave Tom an excellent field for his talents, as well as affording him an opportunity to travel.

France and Germany, it appears, had never settled a disagreement over some African land, and Germany threatened to fight France in order to make her withdraw her claim to this territory. At this time, Tom visited France in the interest of his paper and found that that country was calling for recruits. So impressed was he with the attitude the Frenchmen held towards the Negro soldier,—against whom no discrimination was shown,—that he decided to return to England, resign from his paper temporarily, and enter the French army. Tom had been drilled in military tactics at Oxford, and had hoped for a chance to serve his own country by entering the service at home, if it were possible. His visit to France opened his eyes to the fact that all men were equal in the French army, and his joy at this discovery knew no bounds.

So, into the army he went; promotion quickly followed, till at length, as commander of a regiment, he led a successful charge upon the enemy, sweeping them from their position.

This was a charge that had much to do with the settlement of the question at issue. The territory became the property of the French.

Commander Brinley's fame now resounded through France, and England caught up the strain,—for was it not because of her training that Tom had served so well? Medals of honor were bestowed upon the Negro and he was lauded to an enviable degree.

Tom's mother received from him a letter, in which he told her that he would join the French army and fight, since he could not fulfill his greatest desire,—the serving of his people in his native land. But he added:

"I am serving my people just the same, Mother, by doing something that gives me an opportunity of acting a man's part."

Mrs. Trower did not think so kindly of Tom's adventure, for she felt that if he were to die in battle, every hope that she had fostered for him would be entirely destroyed. When she read of his great achievements, however, her husband remarked:

"Grace, unless you should see the gratitude of France to her warriors you couldn't understand it. It is marvelous how they are lauded. The French worship their heroes as if they were gods."

Tom's chance for making money both in

England and France was now excellent. He received many letters offering him such positions as would have flattered the vanity of many an ambitious youth. This *enbareas de choix* was confusing. Tom was trying to decide just where he would settle and into just which of the open avenues he would turn,—governing his choice always by what he considered would be most agreeable to Mary, whose prayers had followed him in and out of battle,—when he wrote to her that, as soon as he could settle upon one of the many advantageous offers held out to him, she must cross the ocean, and become his wife, according to her promise.

No sooner had he sent his letter off to America than he received a Santa Maria newspaper of recent date, marked with a great cross in ink at the head of a column that read as follows:

GREAT DEMOCRATIC RING OF SANTA MARIA BROKEN —VARDAM'S AND TILTON'S POWER KILLED—REPUBLICAN RULE THE RESULT OF THE RECENT ELECTION—VARDAM AND HIS GANG HAVE BEEN ACCUSED OF GRAFT—MISAPPROPRIATION OF MUCH OF THE STATE'S MONEY.

Then, too, in the text occurred this passage:

After investigation, it was found that through their dishonest maneuvering, the Vance Institute,—that heavily-endowed school for which Enoch Vance so arduously toiled,—had lost everything, and its doors were closed because of the deficit. Who is

there to follow that grand and noble leader and once more
place upon a solid footing this institute, the pride of the
South?

Tom closed the paper, laid it down, and, with
his face buried in his palms, he pondered. At
this moment there came a knock at the door.
He occupied a suite in one of the finest French
hotels. The *garçon,* speaking in French,—
which Tom understood well,—told him that he
was wanted below. Rising, he descended a
magnificent stairway and entered a luxuriously
appointed salon, where a representative of the
President of France awaited him. Tom's
visitor informed him that he was authorized to
offer him an important consulate.

When Tom had expressed his appreciation
of the conference of this great honor upon him,
—he said quietly:

"Duty calls me across the seas to my op-
pressed and forsaken people. I must go and
serve them; I must spend my days in lifting
them out of their igorance, so that their condition may be altered. I thank you for the great
opportunity you have given me to prove my
manhood. To England I owe much, because of
the advantages she gave me of an education
without restrictions. I shall go to my people,
taking those European ideals, which I trust
shall ever be a part of me, and my prayer to
the Almighty shall be for strength to bear un-

complainingly the scourge of prejudice, which, because of unfair laws, has been allowed to run wild in my own, my native land.''

In a few days Tom was *en route* to America. As he leaned over the rail to bid good-by to England and France,—secure in the strength of the glories of centuries,—and afterwards turning his face toward his own land, he said:

''I come back to you, my country, which I love and revere. You have unjust laws; you are unfair to my people; but I believe in your future. I have faith in you, though you mete out partial justice to me and mine, and I shall believe in you as long as I hear Christ's name among you. For through Supreme Love only may I and my people hope for a greater freedom.''

Tom's coming was a surprise to all. And the joy of the Trowers, especially Grace, could not be imagined. They, with the Grants, had hoped that he would find some worthy occupation in Europe; but when they were told of what had occurred in Santa Maria, and of how he was on his way to offer his services to the Vance Institute, with the aim of devoting the rest of his life to the carrying out of the glorious work that the great Leader had started, they could not understand how he could turn his back upon a career rich in honors, in order to serve a hopeless institution.

But without one thought of reward, Tom went where duty beckoned. His mother went with him,—happy to look upon old scenes once more.

As the years went on Tom, with Mary his wife, kept up their zealous efforts in the interest of their people in Santa Maria.

Did he raise Vance Institute to its former glory? Yes, nor was that glory all. He did more; for never again in the history of Santa Maria do we hear of the injustice of the Whites to the blacks—never again did a Brinley, or an Abbott, or any other member of the Negro race, know the ignominy of working in the chain-gang. For Tom Brinley had turned his people's steps away from the rough road of ignorance into the happy highway of hope.

CLOUDS AND SUNSHINE

CLOUDS AND SUNSHINE

BY

SARAH LEE BROWN FLEMING

THIS LITTLE BOOK
I AFFECTIONATELY DEDICATE
TO MY CHILDREN,
DOROTHY AND HAROLD

CONTENTS

CLOUDS AND SUNSHINE

DOROTHEA

The stars in Heaven now shine with a fuller,
    gladder light,
My days no longer seem a long and dreary night;
Since thou dost love me dear, all things seem
    more than bright,
        Dorothea, Dorothea, my own Dorothea.

If griefs and sorrows come, they do not pierce so
    deep,
If tears bedim my eyes they are the bitter-sweet,
If death doth part us here, I know somewhere
    we'll meet,
        Dorothea, Dorothea, my own Dorothea.

And e'en though death does come, I'll always see
    thy face,
Thy hand within my own I ever will embrace,
Remembrance of thee in my soul will have a place.
        Dorothea, Dorothea, my own Dorothea.

[1]

CLOUDS AND SUNSHINE

TUSKEGEE

Sacred spot on which thou art,
    O school of industry.
Thou art doing well thy part
    To aid humanity.

On thy consecrated ground
    Is carved a wondrous story,
Out of chaos, Washington
    Raised this place to glory.

The world has made a beaten track
    Unto thy very door,—
A fountain on the desert sands
    Thou art for evermore.

[2]

CLOUDS AND SUNSHINE

DEATH

The spirit out of it hath flown,
And left the body all alone,
So after all, what is this clay,
Which we so cherish, can you say?

Look on this form now still in death,
The force is gone which we call breath;
The faculties, yes, every one,
Have stopped their use, with spirit gone.

O death, thou art so grim and drear,
What awful silence thou doth wear.
And thou must visit ev'ry one,—
Yes, every being 'neath the sun.

O, death, thou art a woeful state,
All mankind well doth thee berate,—
Because we know not what awaits
Beyond thy grey, mysterious gates.

Ah death, if I could truly say,
"I fear thee neither night nor day!"
If I but knew to what estate
My wandering spirit might awake—

[3]

CLOUDS AND SUNSHINE

I would not quake when thou art near,
Thy presence I would not so fear;
But 'tis the mystery that attends
Thy awful mission, that offends.

[4]

CLOUDS AND SUNSHINE

WHEN LOVE SLEEPETH

Love built a fairy bower, with roses red and white,
And watched it ev'ry hour to keep the flowers
    bright:
For oh, it was so fair, this bower which love did
    make,—
A benediction, prayer, its perfume ever spake.

And when the chill frost came, Love showered
    warmth and kisses,
For whom Love doth caress, the frost he surely
    misses:
But one night Love did sleep, the frost was round
    about,
He pierced the roses deep to blot their sweetness
    out.

Oh, desolation drear hath gripped Love's rosy
    bower,
No brightness find we there, for Love hath lost
    all power,
Ah, Love will sometimes sleep, too oft when
    needed most,
And will not always keep forever at her post.

[5]

CLOUDS AND SUNSHINE

COME LET US BE FRIENDS

Come, let us be friends, you and I,
  E'en though the world doth hate at this hour;
Let's bask in the sunlight of a love so high
    That war cannot dim it with all its armed
    power.

Come, let us be friends, you and I,
  The world hath her surplus of hatred today;
She needeth more love, see, she droops with a
    sigh,
    Where her axis doth slant in the sky far away.

Come, let us be friends, you and I,
  And love each other so deep and so well,
That the world may grow steady and forward fly,
    Lest she wander towards chaos and drop into
    hell.

[6]

CLOUDS AND SUNSHINE

MAN'S INCONSTANCY

The earth revolves,
   The sun doth shine,
The moon at night,
   With stars divine,
All tell us that
   Fond nature's way,
Is much the same
   From day to day.

We know at night,
   When tasks are done,
We'll sleep to wake
   And greet the sun.
We know the spring
   With gentle grace,
To summer will
   Give up its place.

What man is like
   Fond nature true?
Can we depend
   On what he'll do?
Today he steps
   With heavy tread.
Tomorrow finds
   Him full of dread.

[7]

CLOUDS AND SUNSHINE

Today he'll swear
  By all the gods
You can rely
  Upon his words.
Tomorrow, he
  Will say to you,
"I did not speak
Those words untrue."

And so it is,
  From day to day,
We can't depend
  On what men say.
All thro' our lives
  We'll meet but few
Whom we can trust,
  Whose hearts beat true.

[8]

COMFORT

I take my cares to Jesus,
　And lay them at His feet.
He will for every sorrow
　Give consolation sweet.

Upon my head He places
　His hand so tenderly,
He tells me that He giveth
　His love to comfort me.

Oh Christ, Oh Benediction,
　Where could I go for rest,
But here upon thy foot-stool,
　Or else upon thy breast?

Dear Savior, I do feel thee
　Forever at my side;
Take not from me thy presence,
　But with me e'er abide.

[9]

CLOUDS AND SUNSHINE

THE SPIRIT OF A FRIEND

Back to the dust went the dust of the body,
  But the spirit that turned to its Maker on high,
Filled the air, as it passed, with so wistful a
    sweetness,
  That its fragrance will linger through years
    that slip by.

[10]

CLOUDS AND SUNSHINE

MY FORTUNE

A gypsy wandered by one day,
When I was young and blithe and gay,
She begged me in a way so free,—
"Come, have your fortune told by me."

Now certainly, if we could chance,
To know our future in advance,
Would we not think the matter o'er,
Before the gypsy left our door?

Well, this I did, in days before
Experience had taught me; Lo,
I told her I would pay her well,
If she my future life would tell.

I sat me down, and so did she,
My hand she took upon her knee;
"Ah, Miss," said she, "will you but hear,
These rings you have shall cost you dear."

The precious rings I treasured so,
A mother's gift, if you must know.
I said "If these I should not wear
I'll take them off and hold them dear."

[11]

"Ah, no," she said, "that will not do";
I'll hold them for a blessing, true,
And when I give them back again,
The world can ne'er more cause thee pain."

"Gypsy," I said, "I cannot part
With these dear rings so near my heart,
A mother's gift I must retain,
Gypsy, you plead for these in vain!"

She said, "If you'll not give them·o'er,
Ill luck I see for you in store,
Circles around thee do revolve,
In blackness they will thee involve!"

"Give o'er thy rings and thou shalt see
Thy bondage turned to liberty,
Riches and love and fame are thine,
Circles so bright do thee enshrine!"

Her eye was set upon my gold.
Plotting for it her heart was cold;
No sentiment could change her aim,
Her blood was up, for gold she came.

Forgive me, friends, when this I say,
I forthwith gave those rings away.

[12]

CLOUDS AND SUNSHINE

I truly thought she had the power
To change my fortune in that hour.

I've lived to learn since that sad day,
That none can know—whate'er you pay,
Your fortune lies twixt God and you
Who says he knows, he speaks untrue.

[13]

CLOUDS AND SUNSHINE

THE WITCH

Lo, the witch all shriveled and old!
Come in and have your fortune told.
She, by the aid of a magic wand,
Can see the future in your hand.
What in your hand she cannot trace,
She'll surely find it in your face.
She'll tell you when you're going to wed,—
If the friend long gone is alive or dead.
If you'll be poor or you'll have gold,
Come in and have your fortune told!

[14]

PAL, LET'S BE TRUE

Pal, let's be true,
I will, will you?
Our country calls to the strife.
Come to its aid,
Don't be afraid,—
For it to save, what's a life?

Yes, we will go,
Fighting?   Ah more,—
We'll never know a retreat.
Proudly we move,
And e'en will prove,
Our fight the best in the feat.

Wonderful land,
Think of the hand
America takes in the fight.
Hers is to brave,
Hers is to save,
For justice, truth and the right.

[15]

CLOUDS AND SUNSHINE

A NIBBLING MOUSE

The swiftest, nibbling, little mouse,
Has made its home within my house,
I set a trap both night and day,
To try and catch it if I may,—
    This nibbling, little mouse.

Today when writing at my desk,
Out it came to make a quest.
It ran around with so much glee,
Seemed not a bit afraid of me,—
    This nibbling, little mouse.

Straightway I rose and got my broom
To chase the creature from the room.
Round and round it scampered fast;
Trying to catch, I darted past
    This nibbling, little mouse.

We kept the chase up half an hour,
Until I felt I'd lost all power
To chase behind it any more,
So left it prattling on the floor,—
    This nibbling, little mouse.

All tired out, I then sat down
And soon within a study, brown,

[16]

CLOUDS AND SUNSHINE

I thought of phantoms, as they pass,
And how thro' life we chase them as
   This nibbling, little mouse.

Yes, all thro' life we find it so,—
Chasing shadows as we go,
We almost catch them, but alas,
They baffle us and slip on, as
   This nibbling, little mouse.

CLOUDS AND SUNSHINE

BOY AT SCHOOL IN ENGLAND

Mother, could you but know
    What thoughts I have of thee,
Your little boy so far away,
    In this land across the sea.

Mother, could you but look
    Within my eyes so wet
With tears, because I miss you so,—
    This yearning I regret.

Could you but listen as I talk
    Of love and home and you;
My heart so fills I cannot keep
    The grief from coming through.

Last night I dreamed I felt
    Your kiss upon my cheek.
And thought I could not live without
    That touch another week.

The boys around have mothers
    Who see them off and on.
Sometimes I feel so lonesome,
    As if mine were dead and gone.

[18]

CLOUDS AND SUNSHINE

Oh, Mother, it is awful when
  A boy can't have the treat
To see his mother now and then.
  Such luck, it can't be beat.

Say, Mother, won't you promise
  When the next big ship sets sail,
You'll come yourself upon it,
  Instead of sending mail?

[19]

CLOUDS AND SUNSHINE

WHAT IS IT?

There is a subtle something
 That speaks where'er you go,
By tongue it is not uttered,
 Than words it speaks much more.

You go forth on your missions,
 And carry it along;
It's like some beauteous flower,
 And like some soothing song.

It's like some fragrant perfume
 That's wafted by the breeze.
It gives out so much comfort
 It sheds abroad such ease.

What is this subtle something?
 Folks ask me, and I say
I cannot well define it
 Nor either teach the way.

It is an inner something.
 I know that it must be
Clear shining through your body
 And giving light to me.

[20]

CLOUDS AND SUNSHINE

I love to have you near me.
    Just why I cannot say,
But this I know, your presence
    Just changes night to day.

Methought I saw a halo
    Surrounding your fair form,
When you approached that mother
    Whom death had left forlorn.

And then when asked for service,
    As fleetful as a bird,
You answered with a presence
    Which spoke far more than word.

I would, if you would charge me,
    Perform some duty true,
That I may ever daily
    Grow more like unto you.

What is that subtle something
    You carry where you go?
I long to have you name it
    Oh do, that I may know.

[21]

DIALECT POEMS

MAMMY

Large of frame, black of face,
Spotless apron 'round her waist,
Teeth so pearly, eyes so true,
Make you think of heav'n so blue,
       That's Mammy.

Moving 'round the house with ease,
Trying ev'ryone to please.
In and out with so much grace,
Acting like she owned the place,
       That's Mammy.

Sister trudging down the hall
Trips o'er rug and has a fall,
Quick as lightning Mammy's there
Fussing with the hurt and scare.
       Dear Mammy.

Jane has fallen in the dirt.
Soiled all her nice new skirt,
Comes a-cryin' to the place;
Stops soon as she sees the face
       Of Mammy.

[25]

CLOUDS AND SUNSHINE

Mammy soothes the hurt and scare
Till there's none left anywhere,
With her "Hush, now Honey, do!
Mammy loves you through and through."
        Oh Mammy!

Mammy now has passed away,
But the memory lives today
With me, and shall never die,
Though the years go flitting by.
        Blest Mammy.

[26]

DE TANGO LESSON

Start up de ban'!
De men folks stan'
And take yo' partners for dis
    tango-flam.

Now step right so,—
Light on de flo',
    Forward,— an' now backward.
        you all mus' go.

Don' step so hard,
O, bless de Lord!
See Jim done slip like
    de flo' is lard.

Now start again,
I makes it plain,
Forward an' backward
    den ben' yo' frame—

Now do it once mo',
Den I'll say go,—
And' keep up dat move-
    ment all roun' de flo'.

[27]

CLOUDS AND SUNSHINE

Miss Nancy Jane,
Ketch up yo' train!
It mus'n't be a-draggin';
    Does I speak plain?

Look at dem feet,
See how they meet,
No regiment of soldiers
    is got dem beat.

Now ain't dat gran,
Jus' watch Jack Ran,
He's leadin' dem dancers
    like a soldier man!

Look at ole Pop,
Jus' like a top,
I ain't seed him move
    from dat one spot!

Watch sister Cloe,
How she do go,
A-swingin' an' a-swayin'
    jus' watch her on de flo'!

Watch Ephraim's pace,
Now ain't dat grace?
Lor' help me, dese darkies
    is jus' eatin' up de place!

[28]

[194]

CLOUDS AND SUNSHINE

Just' watch dat time,
How dey keeps in line;
Lor' help me, dis music
and dis dancin' is divine!

Ah, let 'er go!
Hear dat music flow,
Dey's playin' dis tango,
like dey ain't no mo!

Look at ole Pop!
Make dat music stop.
He's dancin' like de devil
done nail him to dat spot!

Here, clear de flo',
Sam, ope' de do'.
We ain't gwine to dance
dis tango any mo'.

CLOUDS AND SUNSHINE

BACK-SLIDING LIZA

What's dat Honey, you jis say,
World ain't 'ligious in dis day?
Bless my soul, jis' know dat's so?
I done knowed dat long ago.
Lord dis world does move so fas',
'Ligion now's a thing o' the pas';
Wonder what's the end to be,
I don' know an' I can't see.
All I know I'm satisfied,
Lord I's stickin' on your side.
Dere's my gal,—Liza Jane,
Lordy me, dat gal is vain,
All she thinks about is style.
Lord, dat gal'll drive me wil'.
Talk about your edication,
Lize kin read thro' Revelation,
But her 'ligion's been neglected.
Lize's soul has ne'er been 'fected.
Honey, don't you know dese schools
Never had no kind of rules.
All my money gone to waste
Lize can't pray now, lost de tas'.
What I gwine to do, Miss Ca'line,
Wid dat wayward gal o' mine.
Pray an' it will be alright?
Well, I prays both day an' night,—

[30]

CLOUDS AND SUNSHINE

Lord, do take dis gal o' mine,
In dose mighty hands o' thine.
Shut her eyes to all dis show,—
So invitin' here below.
Show her Lord, de perfec' way,
I done foun' dis many a day.
When she, Lord, Thy love confes'
Shiel' her, Father, on Thy breas'.

[31]

CLOUDS AND SUNSHINE

THE LONESOME MAN

Little Rassus Wickens, sittin' in de do',
Mammy's gone to market, hear him cryin' low,
"Mammy why'd you go an' lef me all a-lone,
I's yo' little Honey, Mammy, come back home."

All de odder chil'n playin in de san'
But dis little darkey is one lonesome man,—
Listen to dose heart-throbs as he cries so low,
Little Rassus Wickens, sittin' in de do'.

Ah, within dat chile-breas', chile of darkes' hue,—
Mother love is dyed in royal color too,
Listen to dose heart-throbs, as he cries so low,
Little Rassus Wickens, sittin' in de do'.

[32]

RACE POEMS

THE BLACK MAN'S PLEA

Chains of bondage did imprint,
Far deeper wounds than one could see.
Sinking through flesh and blood and bone,
They struck the deeper life that is
Beneath the flesh, wherein doth course
The blood that carnal life doth give.
Their piercing darts did wound the life,
That's more than carnal in the man.
Stag'ring underneath the blow,
Which quelled a life-blood for a while,
And which today hath not regained
Its former circulation. Life-blood
That doth make men, men! Not the
Corpuscles of red and white that
Coursing through veins do lend them hue,
But, life-blood that doth give that force
Which makes a glorious race of men,
And fills with pride and all things true,
Giving an everlasting hope!

Prostrate he lay upon his back
Till freedom nursed him back again
To perfect health?—Ah, far from that,
'Tis long 'ere that can be enjoyed.

[35]

CLOUDS AND SUNSHINE

The race, still crippled by the blow
Is like a tree supposed dead,—
Showing now and then some signs of life.
Mankind! no blow is great as that
Which strikes through flesh and blood and bone,
And wounds the vital parts where lives
The greater, nobler life of man.

Ye who look without today,
Upon a race of tardy men,
Whose step is lax and spirit slow;
Although they measure not with those
Who, generations freed, have built
What liberty alone can raise,
Great monuments,—that do proclaim
Much credit to their mighty minds,
Forbearance, do I ask of you.

And do not chide this crippled race
That, convalescent, tries to stand
But totters still from slav'ry's blow.
Tear down your veil of prejudice,
And look ye forth with naked eye
Upon the field of wounded men.
See, some do rise above that plain
Of desolation and despair,
And still go forth with willing hands
To turn the wheels of progress too,
In spite of all that was and is.

[36]

CLOUDS AND SUNSHINE

EMANCIPATION CELEBRATION

Dear friends, we're gathered here tonight,
To celebrate a great birth-right;
Which came to us when Lincoln said
That bondage must be stricken dead;
Or else the country great and grand,
Would totter so it could not stand.
To him appeared in Spirit bold,
The great George Washington of old,
Said he, "This conflict cannot last,
It drains our country's life blood fast.
Haste Lincoln! set these people free,
It is not right, it must not be.

So Lincoln we all know so well,
Did set them free.   Could I but tell
What shouts arose when bonds were broke,
The country trembled at the stroke
When slav'ry fell.   A few remain,
The G. A. R.'s, to tell again
How on the field of fire and blood
They risked their lives, and bravely stood
To help the cause, with all their might.
Dear friends, they are our guests to-night,
Since dear old Lincoln is not here,
They are the next to him most dear.

[37]

[203]

CLOUDS AND SUNSHINE

From slavery forth, without one cent,
With spirit broke, my people went
To wander in the world so cold;
To find a place, and oft were told,
Your pedigree we cannot trace,—
You're classed with an unfavored race.
Forthwith they went with awful taint,
The nature now I will not paint;
The chattels of another race.
O God, 'twas hard to find a place.
Who says the race has not progressed?
He doth not know, we've had the test.

Despite these drawbacks ev'ry one,
We're here to tell what we have done,
And say, if some do not advance
As people do who've had the chance
Of longer years than we've been free.
Just reason why and you shall see.
See what we've done in fifty years!
Another fifty are my prayers
The man unborn will yet perceive
A progress now we can't conceive.

He to the world will then expose,
A worthier race and how it rose.
We've gone part way and I discern
The light of hope as it doth burn.

[38]

CLOUDS AND SUNSHINE

Plod on, my race, to reach the goal;
The path is rough, but that's the toll.
Plod on, to get with all our might,
The things we ought with our birthright!

CLOUDS AND SUNSHINE

RADIANT WOMAN

I passed among the lowly poor,
   Within a little street,
A mother sat within her door,
   A baby at her feet.

In speaking of that mother,
   I cannot say that she
Had pedigree behind her,
   The same as you, or me.

For she was bound in body,
   (As some are wont to say).
Her race, not very lofty,
   Was being crushed that day.

'Tis sad it is the custom,
   In this enlightened time,
That people, not in wisdom,
   Are prone to draw a line,—

And say that human creatures,
   Because their skin is black,
Because they've ugly features,
   Must all be pushed right back.

[40]

CLOUDS AND SUNSHINE

This mother as she sat there,
   Did open up to me,
A realm, so full of grandeur,
   From darkness, oh, so free!

Her face though in its blackness,
   Was radiant as the sun,
Her features, plain and homely,
   Seemed glorious ev'ry one.

What was this revelation,
   I asked myself that day?
That wondrous penetration,
   That to my soul made way?

O yes, 'twas more than human.
   I must in truth admit.
I saw more than the woman
   Who in the door did sit.

I saw that inward something
   A-calling out to me,—
"Look you beyond the body,
   Divinity you'll see!"

The look that was so glorious,
   Transplanted on that face,
Told me a Christ victorious,
   Had in her heart found place.

[41]

CLOUDS AND SUNSHINE

THE DYING NEGRO

Seems to me in lookin' over yonder,
  I see the day a-growin' very dark,
Seems to me while in dis' lan' I wander,
    No joyful song is heard from singin' lark.

Seems to me some lonesome note is stealin',
    O'er barren waste, from achin' people's souls.
Seems to me I hear some lips repeatin'
    "That sorrow in dis' lan' like waves do roll."

Seems to me I hear some distant voices
    Echoin' forth from slav'ry times to me
Seems to me they ask me what I sigh for
    And tells me to be happy 'cause I'm free.

Seems to me I answer an' I tells them
    That slav'ry's chains are broken off my han's,
Seems to me those very chains are bindin'
    My soul so close and closer with their ban's!

Seems to me I hear my people sighin',
    For help, God's help, in dis ungrateful lan',
Seems to me I hear my people cryin'
    "These burdens Lord are more than we can
        stan'."

[42]

CLOUDS AND SUNSHINE

Seems to me the freedom that we cherished
   Is bein' robbed from out our very lives,
Seems to me that which we thought had perished
   Is growin' now to one enormous size.

Seems to me I hear some holy voices,
   A-chantin' now some heav'nly song to me,
Seems to me my soul within rejoices,
   For death at las' has come to make me free!

[43]

CLOUDS AND SUNSHINE

THE BLACK MAN'S HOPE

I hear the talk of the white man's hope
    In the ring and at the poll,
But never a word of the black man's hope
    Do I hear as time doth roll.

Bowed with the weight which slavery left
    Upon his chattled frame,
No star of hope comes into view
    The weight is still the same.

O prejudice, cursed prejudice,
    'Tis thou that blights the way,
And makes us feel there is no hope
    There is no fairer day.

Thou poisoned venom, prejudice,
    Who gavest thee thy birth?
Art born of devil or of man,
    How camest thou on earth?

I've heard it said that some believe,
    That God so in his love
Ordained that man be bound to man,
    Do you believe the above?

[44]

CLOUDS AND SUNSHINE

Do you believe such laws are made
  That blacks should till the soil,
While other races reign supreme,
  Removed from all such toil?

Why, God created all men here
  Upon one level plane.
All bodies of the dust were made,
  To dust must go again.

Then why should color play such part
  Upon this mortal earth?
No man has power to change his skin,
  WE'RE ACCIDENTS OF BIRTH.

[45]

CLOUDS AND SUNSHINE

AN EXHORTATION

Is there no prophet, seer nor bard,
  At this compelling time,
To sing a song or say a word,
  Or even write a line?
Is there an ear that will not hear,
  The wails, the groans of men,
Of suckling infants, babes unborn,
  Oh, who will ease their pain?

Is there a mouth that will not speak,
  Of wrongs they do endure,
No tongues that in a language may
  Some remedy outpour?
Speak, oh, ye long dumb mouths, oh speak,
  And to a people tell
The burden forced upon you now
  Makes earth to you a hell.

A battle fierce is raging,
  Unlike the usual fray,
'Tis worse than other conflicts
  That are fought by night or day.
Those men at last find succor,
  The helpless blind and lame,
But none comes to that woeful depth,—
  The heart, when full of pain.

[46]

CLOUDS AND SUNSHINE

This pain's an awful burden,
    To trudge on day by day.
It crushes soul and body
    And makes indifference play;
It shoots right to the marrow
    Of life, its hopes, and oh,
Threatens the very right to live,
    Tries manhood to o'erthrow.

O bards, who in the days of yore,
    Did move a nation's heart,
Who with your great and glorious strain
    Did still a turbulent mart,
Come sing again another strain
    Of duty, and above
All else, oh, sing that glorious strain,—
    That wondrous strain of love.

Sing them a wondrous story
    This burdened race of men,
Paint it with all the glory that
    Can come forth from your pen.
Set it to tuneful melody,
    As ever man did hear,
So that a race benighted
    Will sing with heartiest cheer.

[47]

PICTURES

I. SLAVERY

Gaze on this picture of the past,
See cruel master, whip in hand,
Upon yon slave, whose back is bent,
Scourge upon scourge he letteth fall.
"My God, my God!" the slave doth cry,
"How long shall I these burdens bear?"
"To work, to work," the master cries,
"Go fill my coffers with thy brawn."
Who doth not know, who hath not felt,
For those who lived in that sad time?
What is the life of him who slaves,
Whose body is not called his own?
They bore the stripes, endured the pain,
With not one murmur but to pray.
They sang the songs we all do know,
The songs that we shall sing again.
These prayers and songs were wafted up,
And, oh, they were so wondrous sweet,
They reached a throne where sits a Judge
Who judgeth slow but judgeth well.
They listened and they heard response—
"I will repay, I will repay!"

II. WAR

Then discord rose twixt North and South,
'Twas over slaves, you know it well.

[48]

[214]

CLOUDS AND SUNSHINE

Came Ab'ram Lincoln to the front,
A bloody battle to pursue.
See war in all its dreadful state,—
A scourge of men these battles are:
A price was paid so dear in blood,
By North and South in that great war,
That not a home was left without
Some loved one gone forevermore.
A cry was made for volunteers
Who'll answer it?   Ah, you can tell.
See black men marching to the front,
With steady step and wondrous stride,
How fearlessly they go to die!
And yet they say we are afraid
To risk our lives for a great cause.
Yet I believe that you or I
If needed at some future time,
Will march as proudly to the front
As they did then in sixty-three.

III. FREEDOM

The war is o'er, the slaves are free,
They walk abroad as man with man.
But note the frown upon the brow
Of yonder man whose skin is fair.
"I will not walk, as man with man,
With yonder black," I hear him say,
"He was not made to cope with me,
Who rule this land, whose skin is fair."

[49]

Then what is this I see unearthed,
So soon as slavery's debt is paid?
'Tis prejudice, cursed prejudice,
Another form of slavery.

IV. LYNCHING

See yonder mob, full fifty strong,
Hound that poor lad of Negro blood.
He fleeth to the woods, and oh,
They set the dogs upon his trail.
At last he's caught, and lo, what then?
They string him to yon leafless tree,
And to his clothes they put a flame,
And now he's in eternity.

V. DISCRIMINATION

Not wanted here, not wanted there,
Such signs go up all o'er the land.
My God, then are my people free!
No vote for you, no vote for me.
Have we not borne the stripes enough,
Our cry goes up,—"How long, how long!"

VI. FUTURE

Let's leave these pictures of the past,
And pictures of the present time,
And wander on and on and on,
Unto some great approaching dawn.
My final picture is this one,

[50]

CLOUDS AND SUNSHINE

'Tis not with master, whip in hand,
But it is Black and White, alike,
Holding aloft the stars and stripes.
They've buried far beneath the sod
Grim prejudice and all lynch laws,
And all in one united band,
Proclaim the freedom of the land.
List, up to heaven there goes a sigh
Of long restraint, and then a cry,—
"Praise God we're free, at last we're free."

[51]

CLOUDS AND SUNSHINE

NIGHT SONG

(NEGRO LULLABY)

I.

Honey, take yo' res, on yo' Mammy's breas',
See dat light a-fadin' 'mong de pine trees in de
    wes'.
Yes, de day is gone, night is comin' on,
Darksome night mus' come to us before another
    dawn.

Chorus

Whippo-will is callin', callin' to his mate,
Mockin'-bird is callin' too,
Pine trees is a-sighin', babies is a-cryin',
As the dark-some night is passin' through.
  Go to sleep, ma little honey, go to sleep,
  Shut yo' weary eyelid an' don' you weep,
    Sleep and take yo' res',
    On yo' Mammy's breas',
  Night can never harm you here.

II.

Honey, don' you see, dat it's got to be,
Day an' night, yes, day an' night, until yo' spirit's
    free,
Den you'll quit ma breas', fer to go an' res'
Wid Anodder, who can pro-tec' you from harm
    de bes'!

[52]

[218]

CLOUDS AND SUNSHINE

PUT AWAY THAT UKELELE AND BRING OUT THE OLD BANJO

I.

Don't you hear old Orpheus calling to you, Alex-
    ander Poe?
He says just quit that ukelele and play on the old
    banjo,
Those Honolulu jingles like the dog has had its
    day,
Go put the faithful banjo down, put the ukelele
    away.
        Chorus:
Way down upon the,—I'm coming, yes, I hear that
    music, oh,
Put away that ukelele man, and play on the old
    banjo.

2.

Put away that ukelele, bring me down the old
    banjo,
Sing again for me the tunes I love, Swanee River
    and Old Black Joe,
Then play for me those melodies my mother used
    to hum,
That between each syncopating note, the banjo
    went "Tum, tum."
        Chorus: Way down upon the, etc.

[53]

ABOUT THE EDITORS

Henry Louis Gates, Jr., is the W. E. B. Du Bois Professor of the Humanities, Chair of the Afro-American Studies Department, and Director of the W. E. B. Du Bois Institute for Afro-American Research at Harvard University. One of the leading scholars of African-American literature and culture, he is the author of *Figures in Black: Words, Signs, and the Racial Self* (1987), *The Signifying Monkey: A Theory of Afro-American Literary Criticism* (1988), *Loose Canons: Notes on the Culture Wars* (1992), and the memoir *Colored People* (1994).

Jennifer Burton is in the Ph.D. program in English Language and Literature at Harvard University. She is the volume editor of *The Prize Plays and Other One-Acts* in this series. She was a contributor to *Great Lives from History: American Women*, and, with her mother and sister, coauthored two one-act plays, *Rita's Haircut* and *Litany of the Clothes*. Her creative non-fiction has appeared in *There and Back* and *Buffalo*, the Sunday magazine of the *Buffalo News*.

Jacquelyn Y. McLendon is Associate Professor of English at The College of William and Mary and has written on the work of twentieth-century African-American writers including Nella Larsen, Jessie Fauset, and Gwendolyn Brooks.